the
DAREDEVILS

ALSO BY ROB BUYEA

What Comes Next

THE MR. TERUPT SERIES

Because of Mr. Terupt

Mr. Terupt Falls Again

Saving Mr. Terupt

Goodbye, Mr. Terupt

THE PERFECT SCORE SERIES

The Perfect Score

The Perfect Secret

The Perfect Star

the DAREDEVILS

ROB BUYEA

DELACORTE PRESS

Text copyright © 2022 by Rob Buyea
Jacket art and interior illustrations copyright © 2022 by Julie McLaughlin

Visit us on the Web! rhcbooks.com

Educators and librarians, for a variety of teaching tools, visit us at RHTeachersLibrarians.com

Library of Congress Cataloging-in-Publication Data is available upon request.
ISBN 978-0-593-37614-0 (hc) — ISBN 978-0-593-37615-7 (lib. bdg.) — ISBN 978-0-593-37616-4 (ebook)

The text of this book is set in 12-point Amasis MT.
Interior design by Ken Crossland

Printed in the United States of America
10 9 8 7 6 5 4 3 2 1
First Edition

Random House Children's Books supports the First Amendment and celebrates the right to read.

For Michael, in celebration of your

best worst ideas and the days

we shared together in the woods

LEAD-IN

It was a simple cigar box, buried many years before we came along. If we hadn't stumbled upon it, maybe it would have kept its secrets until the end of time. But that was not to be.

Whether by sheer accident or the will of the Forest Spirits, as my brother would claim, we'll never know. But we unearthed the box—and after that, everything changed. The Daredevils were born.

A Girl Named Loretta

So much happened over the summer, but some things never change. If you've got a problem with my name, we're gonna take it outside. You'll shut your mouth after I get done slapping the stupid out of you. That's still the same.

It's not like I don't know Loretta is an old-lady name. My father happens to be a huge fan of classic country music, okay, and Loretta Lynn was one of the queens of country back in the day, a real icon, a true inspiration, so I was supposed to be honored. Well, I've got news for you. When you spend your life dealing with people making comments about your name, it's hard to feel that way—cursed was more like it.

My overly agreeable mother was just as much to blame as my father. She let Dad have his way because it was either that or she worried he'd try naming my twin brother Sue. If you don't get that joke, it's because you haven't been tortured by the same music as me. Johnny

Cash, aka the Man in Black, another country music icon, had a famous song called "A Boy Named Sue." Give it a listen. It's all about how a father naming his son Sue made the kid tough because of the obvious harassment the boy had to endure for the rest of his life. If it sounds ridiculous, that's because it is, but don't laugh. By naming me Loretta, my father achieved the same outcome. I had no choice but to sharpen my fists.

Anyways, long story short, I got tagged with Loretta and my brother got stuck with Waylon. Mom thought a modern name like Matthew or Nathan didn't go well with Loretta, so she picked a throwback for my brother too. Dad was thrilled because Waylon Jennings happened to be yet another country music icon, but Mom didn't choose Waylon to please my father. She did it because it was her grandfather's name—my great-grandfather—and he was somebody Mom loved. (More on him later.)

Unfortunately, the name Waylon didn't do anything to help make my brother tough—far from it—but that was okay because I had his back. My brother had been born smaller and weaker than me, so I owed him that much. Say something about me and we'll take it outside; mess with Waylon and I'll stuff your head up your rear end. You think I'm all talk? Just ask Leon Hurd.

A Boy Named Waylon

My mother is a veterinarian, so she's very knowledgeable about animals. She claimed I was an armapossum, which is the combination of an armadillo and an opossum. She reached this conclusion for two main reasons: (1) I'm on the smaller size, fifth percentile for my height and fourth for my weight, and (2) I've got thick skin—like the armadillo. I didn't let teasing bother me. When kids tried to pick on me, I just ignored them—similar to how an opossum plays dead. It was a solid strategy. Eventually, the bad guys left me alone.

Disclaimer: Being an armapossum only worked if Loretta wasn't around, which wasn't often since we're twins.

My sister was a wolf. But not just any wolf. She was the alpha wolf, quick to protect her pack—me—and not afraid of anything. If she was anywhere nearby when the teasing or bullying began, she put an end to it in a hurry— her way, which wasn't always pretty.

Being twins meant Loretta and I had been together since the beginning. All throughout elementary school, she was always there to stick up for me—but that was about to change. Seventh grade would have us attending the middle school, where we might not ever see each other during the day. There were no two ways about it. I had this summer to show my sister I was capable of taking care of myself—so she could stop worrying.

When I was younger, it never bothered me when she came to my rescue, but I didn't always want her jumping in anymore. That being said, I will admit, I was beyond grateful to have the wolf on my side the day I got tangled up with Leon Hurd.

3

LORETTA

Leon Hurd Falls

Leon Hurd was your classic schoolyard bully. He was repeating sixth grade after having already repeated first. It was rumored that he shaved, and that he liked fights. No one knew whether the shaving thing was true, but there was no doubt he liked fights. He was notorious for shouting "Hurd's the man!" after each of his daily triumphs. Everyone was scared of him—until me.

Since Leon was in a different classroom, he and I almost made it through sixth grade without incident, but then the inevitable happened. There was a day near the end of the school year—not that long ago, actually—when all of sixth grade was outside for free time. (Being sixth graders, we were too old to call it recess.) I was shooting hoops on the blacktop, and Waylon was sprawled out in the grass field rereading his favorite book, *My Side of the Mountain,* for probably the hundredth time. I swear, my brother fantasized about being like Sam Gribley, the boy in the story who survives on his own in the Catskill

Mountains for close to a year. Anyways, it was while I was shooting hoops and Waylon was reading when all you-know-what broke loose. Leon didn't see my brother and tripped and fell over him while playing Frisbee. You can bet Leon was madder than a rabid dog after that, especially when he heard kids laughing. He grabbed my brother and yanked him to his feet.

"I'm gonna hang you from the monkey bars by your ponytail, you little twerp!" he roared.

FYI—Waylon's ponytail hung clear to his butt crack. It was beyond excessive, if you asked me, and was the result of his obsession with anything outdoorsman or wilderness-related. (More on that later.)

"But I didn't do anything," Waylon cried.

The instant my brother's voice reached me, I dropped my basketball and took off running.

"Shut up, momma's boy!" Leon growled.

"But I didn't do anything," Waylon pleaded again.

"I said shut up!"

The laughing onlookers grew silent. Things had gone from funny to serious.

"You're hurting me!" Waylon whined.

My brother was in trouble.

"Hey, Leon!" I called as I drew near.

As soon as he turned in my direction, I whipped a handful of dirt in his face—a trick I'd learned from watching Indiana Jones.

"Ahh!" Leon yelled, releasing Waylon and rubbing his eyes.

With the bully blinded and his hands out of the way,

he was no match for me. I kicked him in the shins as hard as I could. He dropped to the ground after two blows—one for each leg.

Waylon ran, but I stepped closer and stood over the pile of wimp. "Hurd's a turd!" I shouted across the schoolyard.

Laughter and cheers filled the air, followed by the repeated echo of my now-infamous victory call.

"Hurd's a turd!"

"Hurd's a turd!"

"Hurd's a turd!" rang over and over.

Leon never told on me because admitting he'd been bested by a girl would've been more embarrassing than getting whupped by one in the first place, and no one else told because they didn't want Leon coming after them—and also because everyone was happy to see him get what he deserved.

The moral of this story: Don't mess with my brother.

4

LORETTA

Head-Doctor's Daughter

Loretta Lynn's most-famous song was "Coal Miner's Daughter." It's still considered to be one of the greatest country songs of all time. It was better than "A Boy Named Sue," I'd give it that, but my praise stopped there. Besides, my father wasn't a coal miner. He was a shrink. A head doctor. A psychologist. A joke and waste of money as I'd heard my jerk gym teacher, P.E. Bubba, grumble too many times—but there was a history there. (More on that later.) For now, let me just say that I disagreed. My father was very good at his job—and I knew because of our frequent chats.

You see, while Mom left the house to go to her veterinarian job, Dad worked from home, so us chatting was convenient—and necessary, he would claim. I won't waste time arguing that point because what's important here is that you understand Dad's office was attached to our house, which was where he saw his patients.

This also explains why my brother and I were regularly and unfairly subjected to his awful taste in music—and terrible singing to boot. Every morning we had to suffer through the likes of Conway Twitty and George Jones, only to be made worse by my father's bellowing as he paraded around the kitchen getting his coffee and our breakfasts together. I would've skipped eating to avoid the torture, but Dad was big on breakfast being the most important meal of the day, so he made us attend before catching the bus. Worst of all was the fact that his position on this matter didn't waver during summer, but thanks to Mom, he did compromise and push the start time back an hour so that we didn't have to get up quite as early. Even so, I was still rubbing the sleep from my eyes when I plopped down at the table on Monday morning.

"Loretta, I'd like to have a chat with you after you're done eating," Dad said, sliding a waffle onto my plate.

Waylon glanced at me from behind his book—Harry Potter #7—and smirked. My brother didn't need as much beauty sleep as me. Enough said.

"About what?" I grumbled.

"Life," he answered.

I groaned and rolled my eyes. "Dad, really? Today is my first day of summer vacation."

"I know. We need to talk about that too."

Waylon snorted, and I flicked a piece of waffle at him.

"Don't think you're getting off so easy, Waylon. We'll be chatting later."

"About what?" my brother asked.

"Your sister," Dad wisecracked. The two of them had a good laugh, thinking they were so funny.

I ignored them and drizzled syrup over my waffle. Silently, I began planning for my chat with Dad. Obviously, he had something he wanted to talk about—but so did I. This was the perfect opportunity for me to renegotiate my summer contract.

My parents weren't any different than most. They were boomers. The whole point behind the summer contracts that they created for Waylon and me was to get us away from technology and screens—and outside, like they had grown up, because somehow that was always better.

I will say, as much as my brother loved adventure and the outdoors, the video game world was still strong enough to suck him in for hours at a time, so the contract was good for him—though I'd never admit that to the boomers.

On the other hand, if we were talking about me, then not so good. Currently, I was limited to one movie or three shows per day. I wanted to push it to two movies or four shows. You see, while Dad's fascination was country music and my brother's was anything outdoorsman or wilderness-related, mine was movies.

The *Star Wars* saga was probably my favorite, but the one that captured our family best was *Back to the Future*. Ever see it? Do yourself a favor and watch the movie before listening to any of the old songs I've mentioned. *Back to the Future* is one of those classics that your parents like to say you must see, except the difference is this one is actually really good.

So my dad played the role of the crazy mad scientist named Doc. Enough said. And Mom played the mom.

Waylon was the nerd, George McFly. And I played the role of Marty—the hero and leader, and George's protector. Just like in the movie, it was up to me to turn things around for Waylon. In the movie, Marty travels back in time to help George. I planned on helping my brother in real time.

You see, being twins meant Waylon and I had been together since the beginning, and this was especially important for Waylon because if it weren't for me my weakling brother might not have survived elementary school—and that truth left me with only one option. There were no two ways about it. I had the summer to toughen Waylon up, because after that we were fresh meat in the middle school, where I wasn't going to be able to look out for him. I might not even see him during the day. As dumb as Leon Hurd proved to be, I knew he wouldn't forget about the embarrassment he'd suffered at my feet, and as soon as he caught Waylon without me around, my brother would be a dead man.

Bottom line: this summer was going to be my most important yet.

But first, my chat with Dad . . .

5

LORETTA

A Summer What?

Our house was actually the same house that my dad had grown up in. My grandparents left it to him in their will. Dad's office was once a sunroom before becoming his bedroom back in the day, and something told me it didn't look any better now than it did when he was a kid. One peek inside and you could see he was in desperate need of an assistant, which was something Mom had been trying to get him to agree to. The place was in complete disarray. He was still working out of the boxes he'd packed from when we moved in two years ago.

"How can you function like this?" I asked, stepping around the mess.

"It might look bad, but I know where everything is," he claimed.

"Is that so?"

"Yes, now have a seat and stop trying to distract me."

Dad pushed a few things out of the way and sat in his armchair while I hopped in the recliner reserved for patients. "You should hire an assistant to help you get this joint under control."

"Now you sound like your mother. Not necessary and not interested," he replied.

"I could do it for . . . let's say . . . fifty bucks an hour."

"I'll keep that in mind."

I watched him pat his pockets and then glance over at his desk. "Looking for something?" I asked.

"Can't seem to find my glasses," he mumbled.

I giggled.

"What?"

"Try your head," I said. "You know where everything is, huh?"

He made a face, then reached up and found them. After he had his glasses situated, we got down to business. "Loretta, your mother and I have talked."

Of course they had. Our chats always started this way. Mom and Dad were an inseparable team, always on the same page. It was so annoying. Next he would mention something about me getting into trouble, and then I would have to remind him it wasn't my fault. He and Mom had gifted my brother with a special talent for building things—traps were Waylon's favorite. You should've seen the shoebox mousetrap he rigged up so that he could catch and release the little critter we had in our last house. The thing involved fishing line and toothpicks and his old Tinker Toys. It looked like an engineering project—and it worked!

But traps aside, Waylon had also inherited a good dose of timidness and absolutely no muscles; me, on the other hand, I was blessed with wits, fast fists, an even faster temper, and the propensity for finding trouble. Dad took credit for my wits—I got them from Mom—but liked to say the rest didn't come from him or Mom, but from my uncle Rusty. Apparently, my father's brother had been a hell-raiser. A real daredevil. The first time my uncle got arrested was for drag racing golf carts on the back nine fairways at the private club where he was working landscape. The next time was for a fight he got in at the county fair after a couple of dudes grabbed his girlfriend's butt. I wished I got to meet him.

Nevertheless, I was mistaken, because the topic of me and trouble wasn't how this particular chat proceeded. Instead, Dad went off course and pretty much endorsed my summer plans, though he didn't know that, and he also found a way to complicate the situation, making it more challenging.

"Loretta, you and your brother will be entering middle school in the fall, and things are going to be quite a bit different for both of you. Not only will you be surrounded by far more peers, but it's also likely you will see little of each other throughout the day."

Tell me something I don't already know, I thought.

"It's time to let your brother grow up and learn to take care of himself. You can't go on protecting him forever. Besides, you want to be known for more than the girl who fights her brother's fights. You need to find your own way."

I shrugged, pretending not to hear that last part. "I could always beat kids up after school instead of during the day," I suggested. "Word will spread and problem solved."

"Problem not solved, Loretta. I'm serious. Your mother and I realize this is no small ask, and that this transition won't be easy for either of you, so to help you prepare and get used to the idea, we've signed you up for a summer camp."

I sat forward. "A summer what?"

Dad opened his mouth to speak, but I didn't let him.

"What kind of camp? Where? And when?"

"Relax," he said. "It's a day camp at the youth center, and it's not every day. Your brother is enrolled in robotics, and we got you registered for the sports group. You'll be at the same camp but not together. Starts next week. It should be a good warm-up for middle school."

Dad continued talking, but what I heard loud and clear was his plea: *You've got to toughen your brother up and get him ready to survive middle school because your mother and I don't know what to do.* The best my boomer parents could come up with was some lame summer camp, which wasn't going to help at all. It was only going to interfere with what I had planned. All of a sudden, I had less time than I'd thought. Never mind renegotiating my summer contract.

"We can talk more later, after you've had a chance to reflect on things," Dad said, giving me one of his shrink lines. "I've got to get ready for my first patient now."

He didn't have to tell me twice. I was out of there. I had work to do.

6

WAYLON

Fraternal Twins

Fraternal twins are the result of two different eggs being fertilized by two different sperm. So while the term "twins" leads you to believe two individuals must be very similar, the truth is, fraternal twins can be as similar or dissimilar as any other pair of siblings. They're only called twins because they inhabited and developed inside their mother's uterus at the same time.

I could've learned all of this from simple internet research, but I got the specifics from Mom and Dad after asking about it one night during dinner. Being a veterinarian and psychologist, my parents liked to talk science, which I appreciated. Of course, once they mentioned sperm and eggs, Loretta lost it. She asked to be excused from the table because it was getting too gross. For being such a toughie, she could be a wimp sometimes.

Anyways, long story short, Loretta and I are fraternal twins—and boy, were we ever different. And I'm not only referring to the fact that I'm a boy and quite a bit smaller than her. There was plenty more. Take our names, for example. My sister was no country music star, or any type of singing star for that matter, so unless you could find me a Loretta who was a champion fighter, I would have to say her name wasn't the best fit—and she would agree. Mine, on the other hand, was perfect.

When we were in first grade, we got assigned a family tree project. The project was made better if you could include pictures and information about family members going back as far as possible, which had Mom digging through boxes of old photos alongside us.

"Here's one of your great-grandpa Waylon," she said after coming across a picture of the old man sitting in his rocking chair.

"The guy I'm named after?" I asked, staring at the photo.

"The guy you're named after," she replied. "Grandpa Waylon had a small house tucked away in the northern forest. My grandma died before I ever came along, so it was just him. Mom tried to get him to move closer, but he never did. Grandpa Waylon was at home with the surrounding wilderness, continuing to hunt and fish and split wood until the day he died. He was what you'd call an outdoorsman, hence his beard and ponytail."

It was a big beard—and I saw his ponytail.

"Grandpa Waylon was always so full of stories and had so much to share," Mom went on. "He'd take me on nature hikes, teaching me all about the plants and animals we saw. I used to love visiting him." Mom smiled at the memory of her grandpa and then continued looking through the boxes.

What can I say, when a seven-year-old boy learns about his incredible great-grandpa who he's named after, he gets excited. That was all it took, and my fascination with anything related to outdoor adventure was born. It was in my blood. If I could've grown a beard to match my great-grandpa's, I would've, but I didn't waste any time getting started on my ponytail. After five years, my hard work and dedication hung all the way to the waistband on my underwear. It was my prized possession.

Dad liked my hair. He joked that I could go on tour singing with Willie Nelson. Willie happened to be a country music superstar with signature ponytails of his own. He was also great friends with Waylon Jennings when Waylon was alive, so Dad's joke made sense for two reasons.

Mom, on the contrary, didn't love my hair, and Loretta hated it. Even so, my sister had still threatened and roughed up more than one kid for picking on me about it, which contributed to her getting the rep of being a bruiser and me a momma's boy. You know what I say? So what if I was quiet and not as tough as her. If they knew she was the one still enamored with her baby blankie, they might change their tune.

Please don't tell her I told you that, she'd beat me up— okay, not really, but she'd want to. Loretta gets really mad about that stuff. Not me. Stuff like that bounces off my armadillo skin—but not the wolf's. It agitates the wolf. And that was exactly how Loretta looked when she emerged from her chat with Dad—agitated.

"You've still got your face in that book," she snarled. "You should just watch the movies."

"Books are better," I countered. "I love how wimpy Neville Longbottom becomes one of the heroes by the end of this one."

"So what you're telling me is there's hope for you yet?"

"What? No. I'm not telling you anything except—"

"Fine. Then I'm telling you there's hope for you yet, but time's a-wastin' and we need to get started."

"Get started with what?"

"Go get ready. We're going to the Millennium Falcon."

7

LORETTA

The Millennium Falcon

The Millennium Falcon was nothing more than a rusty old farm machine, an ancient combine lodged deep in the woods behind our house that had been left for junk long ago—but it was one of our favorite hangouts. Waylon and I didn't get out to it much during the school year, but we spent hours exploring the woods last summer—that was what happened when your parents created a contract limiting your screen time—and the combine was one of our best discoveries. It was mysterious and dangerous, and just plain huge, which made climbing on it a blast. One look at its immense size and odd shape and I named it the *Millennium Falcon*.

We made one other noteworthy discovery last summer when we stumbled upon the signs of a forgotten meeting place tucked away in the middle of a clearing even deeper into the woods. Waylon named the site the Circle of Stones, because as its name implies, we could still see where the large rocks had been arranged in a circle. Most important to my brother, the Circle of Stones was proof that we were on sacred ground.

"Do you know what this means?" he exclaimed. "Early explorers must've been here at one time. They would've positioned their camp near this location."

Waylon believed the spirits of these early forest explorers were always with him in the woods after that. And as he'd soon find out, he'd want their help this summer— we all would.

You see, Waylon and I hadn't made our best discovery yet. That would be happening soon, but first, to the Millennium Falcon. I don't want to get ahead of myself.

8

LORETTA

Getting Started

"What exactly are we getting started with?" Waylon asked, looking up at me as I stood atop the Millennium Falcon.

"Summer," I replied. "We're getting started with summer."

I'd decided the best way to toughen my brother up was to keep my intentions secret. Sort of like in *The Karate Kid*—the original. Ever see it? You need to. It's great. I won't give anything away, but in that movie, Mr. Miyagi, the mentor, has the boy he agrees to train, Daniel, doing all kinds of manual-labor jobs. What Daniel doesn't realize is that the jobs are actually teaching him karate techniques so that he can stand up to his bullies. I needed to come up with my own Mr. Miyagi training plan so that I could put muscles on Waylon without him knowing what I was doing. But how?

"Summer? That's it?" Waylon groaned.

"Yeah, you got a problem with that?"

The kids in school cowered if I ever challenged them like that, especially if I shook my fist in their face, but not my brother. Even if he was a wimp, he wasn't scared of me—which I loved and hated.

"If that's all you've got, then I have an idea," he said.

"Oh, yeah? Let's hear it."

"We're going to build a fort."

"We've tried that before," I grumbled.

"Yeah, but never with this," he replied, waving his hatchet in the air. The silver blade glistened in the sunlight.

My brother had received the small ax for our birthday last month. He'd been asking for it ever since we read the book *Hatchet* in school—which Waylon loved because it was another wilderness survival story. I'd forgotten all about the hatchet, but clearly Waylon had not. The thing was still brand-spanking-new and he was eager to use it.

"You brought that with you?" I said.

"Yeah!" he exclaimed. "I stuck it in my pack with the rest of my survival gear. We've tried making forts before, but today we're going to build the real deal, not some wimpy temporary thing."

I almost laughed in his face, but then it hit me. I didn't care if the fort happened or not, if it fell over or stood strong. If my brother wanted to spend the day wielding his hatchet, then I was going to let him, because that sounded like the exact sort of activity I was searching for. Here was my first Mr. Miyagi training exercise.

"Fine, but I don't want a fort. It needs to be a hideout," I said, playing along. "We've got to keep it hidden from the dark side."

"When I'm done, we can camouflage it," Waylon said. "That'll make it a hideout."

"Perfect," I agreed. "Lead the way."

9

LORETTA

Biceps and Blisters

We left the Millennium Falcon and hiked through the woods until Waylon found what he determined was the perfect area. No surprise, he selected a spot on the edge of the clearing near the remnants of the Circle of Stones. I didn't care. I just wanted him to get started. Biceps didn't grow on their own.

"We're going to build a wigwam," he explained.

"A wig what?"

"A wigwam. It's what some Native Americans made for homes."

It sounded vaguely familiar, but I couldn't picture it. "Can you hide it?" I asked.

"Yes, I'll hide it, don't worry. But first we need to build it."

I stepped out of the way and let him go at it—and go at it he did. Waylon hacked and hacked and hacked. The hatchet was the perfect addition to his survival pack, which, among other things, contained a knife, a rope, and his trusty slingshot. Waylon kept a small pouch of stones in the side pocket on his pack so he could get to them in a hurry if he ever needed to. Like his ponytail, he'd been obsessed with the slingshot ever since first grade, so let me just tell you, my brother had deadly accuracy with the weapon.

My pack was more practical. I had several items, including a flashlight—though I'd never been in the woods in the dark—a water bottle, crackers, and Blankie. If you've got something to say about that, I'll knock your teeth out.

Over the course of the next few hours, Waylon took down several young trees and stripped them of their branches. I busied myself organizing his clippings and clearing the area of any dead limbs and sticks. I was in no rush. Putting muscles on my brother was going to take time. Lots of time. Eventually, though, Waylon set the hatchet aside and selected a sapling from his pile. He took the sapling and stuck one end of it into the ground.

"Now you pull down on the top so the tree forms an arch," he told me while holding the bottom in place.

I tried. I tried hard, but it wasn't working. We needed more help, and in Waylon's case, more muscles. A few hours with his hatchet wasn't enough. I was about to tell him his bright idea wasn't going to work, but I waited too long. My wimpy brother lost hold of his end. The young tree sprang into the air with such force that it yanked me right off my feet. It happened so fast that I didn't have time to catch myself. I flew forward, landing on my face and skidding across the ground on my stomach. Training or not, I was ready to wring my brother's neck. I came up spitting dirt—literally!

"This isn't going to work!" I yelled.

"I know!" he snapped back.

"Isn't there something else we can make? The wigham is too difficult."

"It's wig-wam," Waylon stressed, "and I'm thinking."

I was steaming mad, but I didn't say anything more. I could see he was disappointed and frustrated, and I didn't want him to give up.

"We should be able to build a lean-to," he said after a minute. "It won't be as big and elaborate, but if we do it right, it could still be a great hideout."

"Do we need to bend any trees?"

"No."

"Good," I huffed.

He gave me a dirty look and then began explaining. "First, I need to make a bunch of stakes out of the trees I cut down. After that, we pound the stakes into the ground like we would if building a fence. The stakes need to go from tallest in the front to shortest in the back, so that we have a slightly slanted roof and not a flat one collecting water and caving in on us."

"That would stink," I groaned.

"We follow that procedure to make the two side walls and a back," he continued. "The front stays open. I'll need to add a few crossbeams and corner posts, but you get the idea. Last thing we do is lay a roof."

I shrugged. "Okay." It sounded like more Mr. Miyagi work, so I was all for it.

I stepped out of the way and let him go at it all over again. Waylon chopped and chopped, and I organized the stakes. After another hour of hatchet work and biceps building, it was on to the next step. I was smart and assumed the role of handing the stakes to my brother so that he could do the physical labor of pounding them into the ground.

When all was said and done, Waylon had built a hideout way better than anything I had imagined. It was a legit structure that was rock-solid sturdy.

My brother stood admiring his creation while massaging his forearms and rubbing at the blisters on his hands. Nothing he had ever constructed was better.

I stood back smiling at my own brilliance. If I could keep Waylon doing stuff like this all summer, then he just might be ready for Leon Hurd come school—after his blisters healed, of course. He was beginning to whine like a baby about those now.

"Great work today, young Jedi," I said, giving my brother props. "Next time we'll work on camouflaging the fortress and surroundings to keep it hidden from the dark side."

"Fortress," Waylon mused. "I like that. You hear that, Forest Spirits?! I made a fortress!" he yelled, raising his arms in victory.

I laughed. "C'mon. Let's go. It's almost dinnertime, and I'm hungry."

We gathered our packs and left the woods, Waylon proud and me feeling good about the day's training—but neither of us having any idea of what was to come.

10

LORETTA

Coop's Scoops

Day two of summer vacation began same as day one, with breakfast. Only difference was Mom got to join us at the table because her hours started later on Tuesdays and Thursdays.

"Good morning," the boomers said, greeting Waylon and me when we arrived on the scene. We said good morning back, then sat down and began making our plates. Dad had whipped up a nice spread of eggs and bacon, along with some fresh fruit.

"Who's on your schedule today?" Waylon asked Mom. My brother liked to hear about her different animal patients.

"First up is Diesel," she said. "He's due for his annual checkup. Diesel's a boxer, a nice dog, but he gets upset the moment he lays eyes on me, probably because I only ever see him when he needs his shots."

"Can't blame him, then," Dad said.

"No, you can't," Mom agreed. "I'll have to put a muzzle

on him so that I don't get bit, but that's okay. I'll give him a few treats when we're done, and then we'll be back to being friends."

I grinned.

"Who else?" Waylon asked, reaching for more bacon.

"Well, after Diesel I have an appointment with Chief. He's also due for his shots. I won't need a muzzle for him, but I will need earplugs. He's a tiny dog, and as soon as I poke him with my needle, he'll scream loud enough to break glass. To hear him, you'd think I was sawing his leg off. He's a sweetheart, but a major drama queen."

"And his name's Chief," Waylon said, cracking up. "That's the best!"

I was laughing too. That was funny.

"How about you, honey?" Mom said to Dad. "What's on your schedule? Posting your job opening for an assistant?"

Dad frowned.

"That sounds like a great idea," I agreed. (Mom and I made a good team.)

Dad aimed his frown in my direction after I said that. I smiled.

"I'll get to it when I can," he told us.

"Hopefully, that's soon," Mom replied. "Like, today."

After finishing breakfast and cleaning up, Waylon and I chilled in our rooms. His hands weren't ready for another outing in the woods and I didn't have my second Mr. Miyagi exercise planned, so we stayed away from the fortress. Instead, we hopped on our bikes at lunchtime and made the trip to Coop's Scoops, the best ice cream stand in the county, maybe even the whole state. Besides the creamiest homemade ice cream, they also had a Putt-Putt course, an arcade, and a bunch of picnic tables for outdoor seating.

As expected, it was busy when we got there. Waylon and I waited in line, debating what flavor to get. It was always an easy choice for Dad. He'd pick butter pecan because he knew he wouldn't have to share; nobody else in our family liked that old-person yuck. Boomer! Mom liked to keep it simple. She'd go with their orange-vanilla twist. That was a good choice, but with all the flavors they offered, to pick that every time—another boomer move.

Waylon finally decided on the mint Oreo when we got to the window, but I was still hemming and hawing. Did I want the peanut butter or Heavenly Heath? Thankfully, the experienced scooper saw me struggling and asked me what flavors I was considering.

"Go with the peanut butter," he told me. "It's a great batch today."

So that was what I did. I could hardly wait to taste it. After paying, I grabbed a handful of napkins and turned around to find where Waylon had gone to sit.

Instead of my brother, the first thing I glimpsed was the gleaming red sports car parked with its top down and at a diagonal, taking up two spots in a lot that didn't have enough spaces to begin with. That car was P.E. Bubba's baby—and it was a sight that instantly made anger rise inside me.

The best thing about leaving sixth grade and the elementary school behind was finally getting to say good riddance to that man. Waylon and I would never get stuck with P.E. Bubba again. The guy was the worst of the worst, but I'll admit, his name *was* a good fit. His first name was actually Paulie and his middle initial was E, so he went by P.E., which was perfect for a gym teacher. I also happen to think anyone with the name Bubba should have a belly to match, and P.E. had a winner. I was surprised he could squeeze it behind the steering wheel of his precious sports car. But I could deal with his big belly, it was the stuff you couldn't see that made him despicable.

I let out a low growl and scanned the line behind me, searching for our former gym teacher. You couldn't miss him and his belly—unless you were too busy licking your ice cream cone. Waylon was oblivious to the danger, and there was no time for me to do anything. P.E. bent down to make it look like he was tying his shoe, then stood up and knocked into Waylon's arm just as my brother was walking by. Waylon's ice cream went flying and landed in the dirt.

"Oh, sorry about that," P.E. said. "I didn't see you there."

That was classic P.E. Bubba. He was the sneaky kind of mean that no one else ever saw or that he could claim was an accident when it wasn't, stuff like stepping on your foot or blowing the whistle in your ear—or knocking your ice cream to the ground. The man hated Waylon and me because he hated our dad. Why? Long story short, P.E.

had wanted my mom as his girlfriend back in high school, but Dad got her. (More on that later.) Well, guess what? I couldn't stand him either, and I wasn't about to let him get away with bullying Waylon—because what was my rule? Don't mess with my brother.

I stormed in his direction, but before I got to even the score, Waylon stopped me. "Loretta, let's go," he urged. "P.E.'s an adult and a teacher. You can't beat him up."

"Doesn't matter. He shouldn't get away with that," I snarled.

"Another time," Waylon pleaded. "Let's go."

I hated to admit it, but my brother was right. Assaulting a grown-up in broad daylight probably wasn't a good idea, though a couple of hard kicks to the shins did seem appropriate.

We hopped on our bikes, and I looked back one last time as we were leaving. It seemed no one else cared or had even noticed what just happened—but then who did I spot wearing an orange T-shirt with a lawn mower logo on the front, none other than Leon Hurd. He *was* paying attention. He stood near the picnic tables, staring at me, weed eater in his hands and covered in dirt and sweat. Apparently, Leon was on the landscape crew taking care of Coop's Scoops.

I glared back at him.

Then as Waylon and I pedaled by P.E.'s fancy sports car, the one with its top down, I dropped my ice cream cone on the driver's seat. I didn't even get to enjoy one lick from it—and I didn't care if Leon Hurd was still watching.

11

WAYLON

Mimi's Market

As much as I wanted to get back to the fortress on Wednesday, my blisters still weren't ready. I wasn't sure if Loretta was going to be okay with that, but she didn't have a choice because Dad presented his plans for us at breakfast.

"Okay, team, you've had your fun, so today is a work day."

If he knew about our run-in with P.E. Bubba, he might've reconsidered that statement, but Loretta made me agree not to tell Mom and Dad about our struggles with P.E. a long time ago. My sister liked to handle things on her own. What she didn't like was what Dad had just said.

"What does that mean?" she asked.

"It means you're going to mow the lawn while I send your brother on an errand to Mimi's Market," Dad explained.

Here it was—the beginning of what Dad and I had

talked about. Turns out, he wanted the same thing I did—for me to show Loretta that I could take care of myself and didn't always need her by my side. (Great minds think alike.) By doing so, he and Mom hoped that would also help my sister get a handle on her temper. I wasn't overly optimistic about that. Just look at what almost happened at Coop's Scoops the day before. I did like the summer camp part of Mom and Dad's plan, though.

"Why can't I go with Waylon and you mow the lawn?" Loretta pushed back.

Dad was ready. "Because I have too many appointments and other tasks on my plate—such as posting that job opening you and your mother keep harassing me about—so I need your help. Don't worry, I'll pay you like I always do."

"I want a raise."

Man, Loretta wasn't only tough with her fists, she was a hard-nosed negotiator too.

"How much?" Dad asked.

"It's twenty bucks for the job. Call it inflation."

"Deal," Dad said, winking at me.

She could've demanded twice that, and he would've agreed because executing our plan was that important.

The three of us cleaned up after finishing breakfast, and then Dad met Loretta in the garage with the mower. I jumped on my bike and got out of there before my sister changed her mind and insisted on coming with me.

When I reached Mimi's, I parked my bike in the rack on the side of the store and went inside. The only item on my list was a loaf of Italian bread to go along with the pasta we were having for dinner. That was easy.

I made my way to the back by the deli counter where they kept the bread and rolls—Mimi's made the best sandwiches—and found what I came for. Then I crossed to the other side of the store, near the pharmacist's station, where they had a magazine section. I browsed their selection and found the latest copy of *Scout Life*. I thumbed through it, skimming a few of the articles. It was possible I'd been reading longer than I realized but not long enough to explain Loretta tapping me on the shoulder.

"You're done mowing already?" I said, surprised.

"The mower died after five minutes. The dumb thing's been giving Dad trouble, but he hasn't bothered getting it serviced. It finally quit on him, so now he's got to find a repair shop."

"I bet that made him happy."

Loretta scoffed. "You kidding, Dad never gets mad."

I grinned. That was true, though sometimes I wondered if he really did get mad, maybe a little, but held it in because he was trying to set a good example for my sister.

"Did you get paid at least?" I asked her.

"Heck yeah," she said, showing off her cash. "I was still on the clock."

I snatched the twenty from her hand. "Good, then you can buy me this magazine."

"Ugh," she huffed, following me as we weaved our way to the front of the store, where Daisy was working the lone register. (When you live in a small town, you get to know the people who work in the market on a regular basis. Plus, she also wore a name tag on her shirt.)

There was one woman in line ahead of us. I'm not a big people watcher, but I noticed this lady. She was wearing a bathrobe and dark sunglasses. She had her hair pulled back, but even I could tell it hadn't been brushed in a while. After paying for her things, she muttered a "thank you" and left in a hurry.

"Poor woman. She always looks a wreck," Daisy said as I stepped up to the counter.

"Who is she?" I asked.

"Not sure. She comes here every so often, mostly to pick up stuff at the pharmacy. Is this it for you, just the bread and magazine?"

I nodded and gave her the money.

Daisy rang up my order and leaned closer when handing me my change. "I do know she lives in Old Lady Simpson's place," she whispered. "I saw the address on her pharmacy package the last time she was here."

My eyes bugged. "Thanks," I croaked.

Loretta nudged me forward. "C'mon, let's go," she urged.

I waited until we got outside but couldn't keep it in after that. "Did you hear what Daisy said?" I exclaimed.

"Yeah, I heard," Loretta replied. "And keep your voice down."

"She said that woman lives at Old Lady Simpson's. That house is supposed to be haunted."

"I know. Daisy was obviously pulling your leg."

"You think so?"

"I don't know," Loretta admitted. "That woman sure was scary-looking enough to live there."

"Creepy," I said.

We hopped on our bikes and started on our way, Loretta leading the charge because she was a stronger biker than me. Instead of going straight home, she decided we should swing by Coop's Scoops since we didn't get to enjoy our ice creams the day before and because she had the money from not mowing the lawn. I wasn't sure if I was doing a good job of showing her that I was capable on my own, but I was definitely in favor of the pit stop.

12

LORETTA

Bobcat for Breakfast

"What do you two have planned for today?" Mom asked Waylon and me the next morning at breakfast. (It was Thursday, so she was enjoying her coffee and bagel with us.)

The only response we had for her were a couple of shoulder shrugs. I wish I had a better answer than that—not that I would've told her—but I'd been racking my brain since our first trip into the woods and still hadn't come up with anything for Waylon's next training exercise. Camouflaging our fortress wasn't going to be enough on its own. How did Mr. Miyagi do it?

"Those blisters are looking better now," Dad said, noting Waylon's hands. That was what happened when your father was a shrink. He was trained to make astute observations and pick up on subtle details. I was actually surprised he hadn't said anything sooner. "So maybe another day exploring the forest," he suggested.

Waylon and I exchanged a glance. We'd agreed not

to say anything about the fortress. It was our secret hideout.

Mom and Dad, the opposing team, exchanged their own glance. They were onto us.

"What do *you* have planned?" I asked Mom, hoping to shift the spotlight to her.

"I have a date with Buster, the golden retriever who got into a tussle with a porcupine—and lost," she said, letting us off the hook—for now. "I had to remove over a dozen quills from his face and paws yesterday. Poor guy was in some rough shape."

"Is he going to be okay?" Waylon asked, genuinely concerned.

"I think so, as long as his wounds don't become infected. He'll be sore and only eating soft foods for a while, but better he learned his lesson from a porcupine than that bobcat we've been hearing about."

"Bobcat?" Waylon repeated, perking up.

"Yes," Mom confirmed. "There have been at least three different sightings, but don't worry, it's not near us. At least not yet."

"Wow," Waylon muttered.

Who was she kidding? My brother wasn't worried, he was fascinated. I could read his mind. He didn't have any buffalo to hunt from the Wild West days, so a bobcat could be the next best thing. Getting Waylon ready for middle school was going to be hard enough; I was not encouraging any lunatic bobcat hunt.

"How about you, Dad?" I asked, getting us off that

subject. "Do you have a date with cleaning your office, I hope."

Mom laughed.

"Funny," he replied. "I have a few patients to see and phone calls to make, but I save the dates for my beautiful wife." He strode over and planted a big wet one on Mom's lips.

"Gross!" I groaned, shielding my eyes. "Too much PDA!"

"How do you think we were made?" Waylon said, which only made it worse.

"Stop!" I yelled. "I don't want to think about that."

Mom and Dad laughed. What can I say, they were boomers and lovebirds—ugh! Their morning love affair didn't help me focus and devise a training plan, I can tell you that. I had hoped something would come to me before we finished breakfast and went about our days, but that didn't happen. In fact, by the time Waylon and I were on our way to the woods, the only idea I'd come up with was trying to trick him into carrying a couple of large rocks to our new hideout so that we had a place to sit. I was no Mr. Miyagi.

"So, young Jedi, what's the plan for hiding our fortress?" I asked him after we'd reached the lean-to. Maybe I'd figure out what to do next while working on this first task? Or maybe my brother had more planned than I realized? After all, his brainiac idea had led to the first great day of training.

"First, we need to—"

He stopped short. "Need to what?" I said.

"Shhh!"

"Don't shush me," I snapped.

"Shhh! Listen," he urged.

I heard it. Something was approaching, and it wasn't walking lightly, nothing like a hunter tracking its prey—which meant silent, as Waylon was always telling me. This thing made enough noise for a herd of elephants. Sticks and twigs snapped and popped under its every step. Whatever it was, it wasn't small.

Waylon handed me his hatchet and loaded his slingshot. "Whatever comes through those trees is gonna get it right between the eyes," he whispered. "When it goes down, you finish it off with the hatchet."

"Eww," I whined.

"Maybe it's the bobcat," he said, sounding excited. "Forest Spirits, guide my stone with deadly accuracy, and I promise to pay your creature its proper respect."

"Forest Spirits, make it go away," I pleaded.

The creature grew closer.

Closer.

Closer . . .

13

WAYLON

Louie

A large boy crashed through the trees and stepped into view. He was bigger than Loretta and me. Bigger than Leon Hurd even, but less muscles and more pudge. More important, he was decked out in green-and-black camouflage from head to toe, backpack included. There was only one explanation: he was an obvious friend of the army's. But was he friendly? He didn't appear to be threatening. I lowered my slingshot.

Loretta wasn't convinced. Still holding my hatchet, she jumped in front of the boy. "Halt! Who goes there?" she thundered.

"Ahhh!" he screamed. She'd scared him so bad I was surprised he didn't wet himself.

"State your name, soldier," she ordered.

"Umm . . ."

"Your name is Um?"

This poor kid was no match for my sister.

"No," he croaked.

"Then what's your name?" Loretta demanded.

"Louie."

"Louie what?" she pushed.

"Louie Foster."

"Where are you from, Louie Foster?" She wasn't letting up.

The boy pulled an inhaler from his pocket and took a puff. "I live on the other side of the forest," he rasped.

"Why haven't we seen you before?"

"I'm homeschooled," he replied.

"Okay," I said, stepping in and coming to the boy's rescue before Loretta ate him alive. "Hi, Louie. I'm Waylon, and this is my twin sister, Loretta."

"Loretta?" he repeated, which was the definite wrong thing to say, especially in that incredulous voice.

"Yeah, you got a problem with my name, soldier?" Loretta growled, getting up in his face.

I took my hatchet from her before things got ugly.

"No problem," Louie squeaked, shrinking back.

"No problem, sir!" Loretta ordered, her voice rising.

I looked at her sideways. Had she lost her mind?

"But you're a girl," Louie said.

This kid was a slow learner. Did he have a death wish?

"So now you've got a problem with me being a girl? How about I fix that right now," Loretta said, pounding a fist into her hand for emphasis.

"No, sir," Louie said.

"I can't hear you."

"No, sir!" he shouted.

"That's right, soldier. You best not have a problem.

Luke Skywalker and Han Solo needed Leia, Harry and Ron needed Hermione, and you and Waylon definitely need me."

"Need you for what?" I asked.

She glanced at me and smirked. We were in trouble.

14

LORETTA

Hooah!

I didn't know what I was doing, but I was having fun making it up on the fly.

"Attention!" I ordered. I was getting good at this army sergeant thing.

Louie brought his heels together and saluted. I glared at my brother. Waylon shrugged and then followed suit, ready to play along. Even standing tall, Waylon only came to Louie's chest.

"How long have you been growing your ponytail?" Louie asked my brother while trying to keep his voice low.

"Since first grade," Waylon answered.

"It's a bit much, don't you think?" I interjected.

"No, it's impressive," Louie replied. "I mean, no, sir! It's impressive."

"Thanks," Waylon said, and grinned. "My great-grandfather had one, and I'm named after him."

"That's cool," Louie said.

"Attention!" I ordered, refocusing my troop. "Men, we have this fortress"—I gestured behind me—"and it needs hiding. Captain Ponytail, is that something you and Captain Camouflage can handle?"

Waylon stepped forward. "Sir, yes, sir!"

"Explain," I said.

"Sir, we need to take the trimmed branches from the other day and weave them in and out of the posts along the sides and the beams across the top. But, sir, we'll need more to finish the job."

"Good plan, Ponytail. I'll get started weaving while you and Captain Camo go and collect more branches."

"Hooah!" Louie shouted.

Waylon snickered. Even I had to bite my cheeks to keep from laughing.

We saluted, and then my two soldiers marched off. Somewhere along the way, we'd gone from being Mr. Miyagi and Daniel to playing the roles of Lieutenant Dan and Forrest Gump from the movie *Forrest Gump*. Ever see it? It's the best. Or maybe I was Mulan? Either way, I was in charge and my orders were being followed. Sometimes you just have to go with the flow.

I got started bending and wrapping the small branches around our fortress. Before long, my two soldiers returned with additional trimmings, and we worked together to finish the job. When done, we stepped back to assess our work.

Louie took another puff from his inhaler. "It looks great," he said. "Did you build it all by yourselves?"

"A few days ago," Waylon answered. "Do you have asthma?"

"Yeah," Louie said. "I could never build something like that," he admitted.

"Thanks," Waylon replied, swelling with pride.

If I wasn't mistaken, these two were already becoming friends. Keeping them together seemed like the smart thing to do. Training alongside a teammate definitely made it easier, and besides, it looked like Louie needed just as much toughening up as Waylon—maybe more.

"Men, it's time to hold our first meeting," I announced.

"Meeting for what?" Waylon asked.

"The first meeting of our brand-new club."

"But we don't have a club," he pointed out.

"We have a well-hidden fortress and we have three people, so we do now," I countered.

"What kind of club?" he asked next, persisting with his many questions.

A gonna-make-you-tough club, I wanted to say, but I bit my tongue. "I don't know yet, but that doesn't matter," I said instead.

"Um . . . Sergeant, sir," Louie said, "I want to be in your club and do your meeting thing, but I need to get home."

I sighed. "It'll only take a few minutes," I said.

"No, you don't understand. I need to go now," he insisted. "I've already been gone too long. If my mom realizes I'm missing, it won't be good."

I glanced at Waylon, wondering if he also found this peculiar.

"Okay, Captain Camo. Understood. We'll follow you

home in case you need backup," I suggested. (That was more of me making things up on the fly.)

Waylon nodded, showing he agreed.

"Um, okay, but you can't let my mom see you," Louie warned. "You have to stop at the edge of the forest and stay hidden."

Now, that *was* peculiar.

"Affirmative," Waylon replied, and saluted.

"Move out," I ordered, growing more curious by the minute.

15

LORETTA

Louie's House

It was a fair distance to Louie's side of the forest. As much as Waylon and I had explored the woods, we'd never ventured this far. I wasn't sure where we were going to come out until we got there—and then I knew exactly where we were.

"This is your house?" Waylon asked, incredulous. He knew where we were too.

"Yeah. We moved in last summer."

Waylon and I locked eyes.

"Oh no. I'm too late," Louie groaned. "It looks like my mom's already awake. I'm a dead man."

"Your mom sleeps during the day?" Waylon asked, taking the words right out of my mouth.

"Sometimes," Louie replied. "I've gotta go."

Waylon and I watched as Louie stepped out of the forest and hurried across the backyard leading up to his house.

"Do you think that tired-looking lady we saw at Mimi's is his mom?" Waylon asked, keeping his voice low.

"Maybe," I whispered.

"I can't believe he lives here."

"I know."

Everyone knew this house, the one that had belonged to Old Lady Simpson. When she was alive, Old Lady Simpson had the place lit up like a stadium every night. And I'm not talking your normal house lights and lamppost. There was that, but she even had lightbulbs in the trees. Legend had it the property was haunted and she used lights to ward off the demons. After she died, the place sat in the dark until Louie's family moved in. But here was the thing: no one ever saw Louie's family, so the legend only grew. People said it was Old Lady Simpson's ghost that had come back to turn the lights on. Creepy stuff.

Louie reached the door and slowly turned the knob. Waylon and I crouched in the bushes, holding our breaths, waiting to see if anything happened. We didn't have to wait long. Louie pushed the door open and carefully stepped inside. His mother's hysterical cry immediately followed, slicing through the air and sending a shiver up my spine.

"Where have you been?!" she shrieked.

The wild-eyed woman stuck her head out and scanned the yard, then slammed the door shut. It *was* the same lady.

"Whoa," Waylon muttered.

"Whoa is right."

"Let's get out of here," he urged.

"Wait."

"Wait? Wait for what? Did you see that lady? She's crazy."

"Just wait," I said.

Waylon huffed and gave in, but after a few minutes of nothing, he was done cooperating.

"C'mon, let's go," he urged again. "Nothing's happening."

"There!" I exclaimed, pointing. "That's what we were waiting for."

Louie's face appeared behind one of the upstairs windows. "That must be his bedroom," I reasoned. "We needed that piece of information for when we come back to sneak him out."

My brother's eyes grew wide. "Sneak him out?" he repeated. "When?"

"Not right away. We'll wait, give his mother a chance to cool off. We've got that dumb camp to go to anyways. But after that, we strike. We'll come at midnight."

Waylon swallowed. "Midnight?"

"Yes, midnight. It's always at midnight in the movies, and besides, he'd never escape during the day, not now. You want adventure? Here it is."

Waylon swallowed again. "Okay," he croaked. "But if we're doing that, then we need to go back and build a firepit. We're going to need it."

And there it was. Building a firepit meant digging and hauling rocks. I had my Mr. Miyagi exercise.

"Move out," I said.

16

LORETTA

My Penalty Kick

After a rainy weekend and wet and boring Monday, the sky cleared and the sun came out just in time for the thing I was most dreading.

"Is my dynamic duo ready for camp?" Mom asked at breakfast. Conveniently, this dumb camp thing was happening on Tuesdays and Thursdays, so she was able to drop us off before going to work.

"Oh, yes. Thrilled," I groaned.

"Yeah," Waylon replied, sounding sincere.

I shot him a glare. Was he playing kiss-up or being serious?

He just shrugged, acting like this wasn't going to be terrible. Well, he was wrong.

The whole camp ordeal was made even worse the moment we pulled into the parking lot and I saw who the director was. Standing in front of the youth center, greeting everyone as they arrived, was none other than P.E. Bubba.

"Are you kidding me? P.E. Bubba," I groaned.

"I know," Mom said. "I'm sorry. But he's only the director, so it's not like you'll have to see him all day long. Once you split into your groups, it'll be fine."

She was apologizing and claiming it'd be fine because she knew firsthand how terrible this man was. You see, once upon a time, P.E. was the local sports hero, if you can believe that, but the only thing he could never win was my mom. She was Dad's girl. The two of them fell in love when they were lab partners for a genetics unit in biology. Playing with fruit flies and making fruit fly babies must've been romantic because that was all it took. Boomers! As Mom tells it, she wasn't interested in P.E.'s muscles and bullish attitude; it was Dad's sensitive and inquisitive personality that won her over. (Does that sound like Waylon or what?!)

Unfortunately, P.E. didn't take losing well, so he started bullying and harassing my dad. The harassment continued until Uncle Rusty caught wind of it. Uncle Rusty had already graduated but was still hanging around—trying to find his way was how Dad described him. (Sound like familiar words?) Well, after catching wind of it, my uncle decided to pay P.E. a visit in the student parking lot one day after school. As Mom tells it, Uncle Rusty taught P.E. a hard lesson—in front of many spectators. Mom says P.E.'s pride was what got hurt the most. The legend of the local sports hero was forever rewritten that afternoon. Guess you could say Uncle Rusty was looking out for his little brother. (Sound like anyone you know?)

Anyways, getting back to me and my problems. Waylon and I grabbed our bags and got out of the car. Waylon said bye to Mom, but I didn't. I wanted her to feel my extreme displeasure—with her and this camp situation. Of course, if she and Dad knew the half of what Waylon and I had experienced with P.E. Bubba, they might not have sent us to this camp in the first place, but we never told them, so that was on me. There was no point in telling because there wasn't anything my parents were going to be able to do. We couldn't prove anything, because like I already told you, P.E. was too sneaky. It would be our word against his, and that wasn't going to end well. Waylon and I had inherited P.E.'s harassment same as you inherit your genes from your parents. But remember, I'd also been gifted with a good amount of my uncle Rusty.

The two of us walked to the side of the youth center building where everyone was meeting and waiting for things to get started. The youth center and surrounding fields and courts and playground areas made up a big campus, and there were kids spread out all over the place. We hung out, avoiding P.E., until things got underway.

First thing P.E. did was blow his whistle and bellow for everyone to "get over here!" He went over a few rules and then introduced the many counselors working at the camp. After that, he sent the different groups to their various locations. Waylon was lucky and got to run off to a building across the street with his robotics bunch and some geeky math teacher from the high school—but better me than my brother left to deal with P.E. Bubba. I could handle myself.

As luck would have it, and just to make my camp

matters worse, because Dad had signed me up for the sports option, I got stuck with P.E. as my instructor. There were counselors on hand who were ready to assist, but since this was day one, the big man was running the show and acting all important.

P.E. blasted his whistle a second time and gathered his sport campers on the field behind the youth center. "Well, well. If it isn't the loser shrink's daughter," he grumbled under his breath after noticing me. Making sly comments that no one else understood or heard was another one of his sneaky mean tactics. "Is Pipsqueak Ponytail here too?" he asked, and smirked, knowing how to push my buttons.

I clenched my teeth and bit my tongue, but that didn't mean I was letting him get away with trashing my father and brother. Fat chance. Two could play his game.

P.E. took attendance and gave us his pep talk, then dumped a bag of soccer balls on the ground and told us to warm up. I dribbled around for a few minutes, but as soon as P.E. was done chatting with his counselors and was left standing alone and not paying attention, I let one of my penalty kicks fly. He was lucky his belly was as large as it was; otherwise my shot would've drilled him you know where. It still dropped him to his knees. Anyone who saw it was laughing, which infuriated P.E. I bet getting laughed at brought back bad memories for him.

He fixed his shirt and hat and got to his feet. I didn't even try to hide. I stood my ground and met his angry glare. "Sorry. That one got away from me," I said.

"You're out!" he roared. "You can stand against the wall for the rest of the day. In the sun!"

The wall was the back of the youth center building, where there was no shade. Fine. I didn't care. It was worth it. Besides, I expected the punishment. What I didn't expect was what happened next.

"She got you good, huh, P.E.?"

"You think that was funny, Hurd?" P.E. snarled. "Well, guess what? You can join her."

"I don't think so. I'm not one of your campers." Leon fired up his weed eater and continued trimming the grass around the border of the playground area. Apparently, the landscape crew he worked for took care of the property at the youth center, which was why he was there.

And so there you have it. That was how I wound up standing against the wall in the blazing sun, watching the kid in the orange T-shirt with the weed eater. I could see Leon's muscles glistening with sweat from across the field. The way that boy was constantly working, he was only going to get bigger and stronger, which meant I wouldn't be so lucky a second time around. I didn't expect him to fall for the dirt-in-the-eyes stunt again. Just because he'd been held back twice didn't make him dumb. But I did expect a showdown. It seemed inevitable, like Luke Skywalker facing off with Darth Vader—only I didn't see any surprise twist in our saga.

17

WAYLON

Keeping Camp Secrets

I found Loretta after camp, and we made small talk while waiting for Dad to pick us up.

"How was your day?" my sister asked.

"Good," I replied. "Yours?"

"Boring."

We left it at that. It wasn't hard to keep Loretta from asking questions and wanting more details because something told me she wasn't telling me everything either—and that was fine. It seemed we had reached a silent agreement to let one another keep camp secrets. However, that agreement didn't prevent Mom and Dad from asking questions at dinner later that night.

"So how was camp?" Mom asked when we were all seated around the table.

Loretta and I exchanged glances. "Boring," she answered.

Mom looked at me next.

"Good," I replied.

The two of us were sticking to our stories.

"Really? That's it?" Dad said. "Boring and good. That's all you can say?"

Loretta and I looked at each other and shrugged. "Yeah," we said.

"I'll take it!" Dad exclaimed, startling us. "You survived the day without being together, which is exactly what this camp experience is meant to show you. Preparing you for middle school, remember?" He winked at me.

I smiled. I couldn't help it. Loretta, on the other hand, scowled. If she knew the truth, that camp had been a lot of fun for me, that I'd made a friend and couldn't wait to go back on Thursday, I imagined her scowl would've been even deeper—which was why I wasn't telling her.

"How was your day, hon?" Mom asked Dad next.

And on that note, the conversation moved on. Dad shared that he had a few job applicants already, which excited my sister and Mom, and Mom told us about two different cats that she'd seen. I liked her dog stories better.

Following dinner, Loretta told me to meet in her bedroom. I guess mine was too messy. My sister wasn't interested in talking any more about camp; we had far more pressing issues—namely, discussing our sneak-out mission. We agreed that Louie's mom still needed time, so we decided to dedicate our Wednesday to devising our exact plan—one that had to be carefully thought out and detailed. Thursday would be taken up by camp again, so the decision was made to make Friday the night we put our plan into action.

I had so much to be excited about that it took me

extra long to fall asleep that night. Plus, I was also a little nervous about going back to Louie's house—but I wasn't about to tell Loretta. Not if I wanted her to see me as able to take care of myself. The only thing I could do was hope the Forest Spirits were with us when it came time.

18

LORETTA

Getting Louie

One advantage to having boomers for parents: they went to bed early. And that was a helpful fact when it came to sneaking out.

Waylon and I were so anxious when Friday night finally arrived that there was no chance either of us was falling asleep. We were about to embark on a dangerous expedition. One that not only involved sneaking out but also rescuing a fellow soldier from captivity—a prison break! Add to that the risk of getting caught by the crazed patrol woman—Louie's mom—and you had the stuff of a high-adrenaline action movie.

At the stroke of midnight, we put our plan into motion. Not only was midnight when things of this sort always happened in the movies, but we also needed it to be dark, and the later the better because then there was less chance of us being spotted. This was especially important because Waylon and I had made the risky decision to travel by road until we got closer to Louie's house, and then we'd duck into the woods.

Why take that chance? Because Louie's bedroom was on the second floor, which meant we had to lug Dad's ladder with us; otherwise we'd never be able to break him out. Let's face it, Louie wasn't the type of kid who'd tie his bedsheets together and climb down. Not happening. Carrying Dad's ladder wasn't going to be easy to begin with, but trying to do it through a pitch-black forest would've been near impossible. If a car happened to be driving by at that hour, then we'd just have to do our best to hide in the ditch or wherever we could. There was a certain amount of risk one had to take when embarking on a mission of this caliber.

When the time finally came, Waylon and I met outside, both of us dressed in black sweat pants and dark-colored hoodies and two pairs of socks—the extras would be needed soon. We had our survival packs and headlamps, a Christmas gift from last year that seemed silly at the time but were going to be invaluable to us now. First stop: the garage.

We snuck in through the back door, which I'd made sure to unlock earlier in preparation, and gently lifted Dad's ladder off the wall, one of us at each end. Carefully, very carefully, so as not to make even the slightest sound, we carried it out. One slipup, one bump into anything that made a noise and our mission would've been in jeopardy before it even got started.

Once outside, Waylon took the front, and we double-timed it down the road. We were sweating and breathing heavy when we reached the spot where we took cover in the woods, but we got there before any cars drove by, which was good. We weren't far from Louie's now.

Having Waylon in the lead was smart and helpful because he was the best at picking a path through the woods—but doing so in the middle of the night was a challenge for even the most-experienced outdoorsman. Our headlamps provided minimal help. We actually bene-fitted more from the full moon hanging high above. But here was the thing: there's a reason why a forest is said to come alive under a full moon—because trust me, it was alive! I could hear owls hooting. Frogs croaking. And lots of rustling. The chorus of eerie noises seemed to be com-ing from everywhere—and closing in! Being quiet was important, but our pace quickened because staying alive was more important. What if the bobcat was stalking us?

Needless to say, my nerves were fried when we fi-nally reached the edge of the forest in back of Louie's house. Waylon and I crouched behind cover, taking time to check our surroundings and slow our racing hearts. Our breaths danced on the night air as we took off our extra socks and retied our sneakers. One thing about the country, even summer temperatures dropped enough to make it chilly after the sun set.

I surveyed the scene once more. "You better take those two out," I whispered, pointing to the lights in the trees nearest to the path we'd be taking.

Waylon nodded. He loaded his slingshot and fired one stone and then another. Two shots and two lights knocked out. Told you he had deadly accuracy with that thing. I had been worried about how much noise breaking the glass would cause, but thanks to Waylon's clean shots it was minimal.

"Nice work," I said.

"Thanks."

"You ready?"

"Let's go," he replied, grabbing his end of the ladder.

We'd gone over our plan from this point several times so that there'd be no need for talking. Silence was our best weapon when attempting a prison break.

We leaned the ladder against the house directly under Louie's window. I nodded at Waylon, and he handed me his extra socks. I balled them up, took two steps back, and fired my first sock bullet at Louie's window. Bull's-eye.

Waylon retrieved the ammunition after it fell back to the ground, and I prepared a second bullet, using my extra pair of socks this time. Again, I took aim and fired, bouncing another shot off the glass.

Waylon tossed the first bullet back to me, and I chucked it up there again. Louie opened his window and stuck his head out just as my fourth throw went flying. I hit him right between the eyes.

"Sorry," I mouthed.

"Are you crazy? What're you doing here?" he whisper-shouted.

I put a finger to my lips to silence him, and Waylon scurried up the ladder to explain. The last thing we wanted was a lengthy back-and-forth conversation.

After hearing what my brother had to say, Louie gawked at me like I really was crazy. I beckoned him with an energetic wave of my arm. His eyes grew wider. Waylon said something else to him and then came back down.

"Well," I said. "Is he coming?"

Waylon shrugged.

That wasn't good enough. "This is exactly why you can't send a boy to do a woman's job," I huffed.

I sprinted up the ladder. After what we'd already done for him, I wasn't letting Louie off the hook. I was prepared to drag him out that window if I had to, but I wasn't prepared for what I saw. When I got to the top and peered inside, Louie was changing out of his camo pajamas and into his everyday camo attire. The only not-camo on him were his tighty-whities—which I didn't need to see! I averted my eyes. When I glanced at him again, he was dressed and pulling on his backpack.

Louie waited for me to climb down, then gave a last glance over his shoulder and started his descent. Waylon and I steadied the ladder. As soon as Louie hit the ground, we turned and ran. This was not the time or place for small talk. We left the ladder where it was, knowing we'd need it when we returned. Waylon led us all the way to the Circle of Stones before we finally stopped. I wasn't about to let him stop before that. There was no way I was giving the bobcat or any animal lurking in the dark the chance to pounce on us!

19

WAYLON

Our First Fire Ceremony

Louie took a couple of puffs from his inhaler and then began freaking out.

"This is crazy!" he exclaimed. "What're we even doing here? If my mom—"

"Welcome to the Circle of Stones," I said, gesturing to the sacred site Loretta and I had resurrected, a total of thirty-seven large rocks surrounding a central firepit. "Tonight we hold our first fire ceremony, to honor the Forest Spirits and this hallowed ground."

I didn't know if Loretta had a plan, but I was taking over. This was my area of expertise. I pulled Dad's newspaper and a lighter from my backpack and knelt next to the pit. Loretta and Louie watched me twist and wad the sheets of newsprint, adding it to the firewood and kindling I'd already assembled.

"When did you build this and get everything ready?" Louie asked.

"We came back and did it after dropping you off at home the last time," Loretta explained.

I flicked my lighter and touched the flame to the paper. Within seconds, my fire began to grow. I stood and stepped back from it.

"Whoa," Louie wheezed. "You're just as good at building fires as you are fortresses."

I lifted my palms and chin to the sky and spoke. "Forgive me, Forest Spirits. Using a lighter and paper is cheating, but we only have so much time."

Loretta scoffed. "They forgive you," she said. "If anything, they're impressed. Trust me, if they had a lighter back in the day, they would've used it."

"Who're the Forest Spirits?" Louie asked, confused.

"The brave men and women who explored these woods long before us," I explained. "Tonight we summon their spirits from the past. We ask them to be with us, protect us, and guide us as we continue our quest."

"What's our quest?" Louie asked next.

"We don't know yet," I admitted, "but with the help of the Forest Spirits, it will become clear soon enough."

His questions stopped for the time being, but there'd be more from Loretta and him after I proceeded. That was okay. I dug through my backpack and pulled out the other materials that I'd brought with me: a variety of markers, different colors and styles, some permanent and some washable, a packet of alcohol wipes, and three pieces of paper, each containing a unique and important picture.

"What's all that for?" Loretta asked.

"There are two main requirements for any fire ceremony," I explained. "The first involves giving each other tattoos, and the second is a dance."

"What?!" Louie yelped. "I can't go home with a tattoo! You've lost your mind!"

"We must!" I exclaimed. "A proper fire ceremony is the only way to summon the Forest Spirits. We have to do it, or we risk offending them, which would not be the wise thing to do."

"Relax, soldier," Loretta whispered to Louie. "They're just markers."

Louie's whimpers quieted, and I pressed forward. Since Loretta was acting brave, I started with her first. I stepped in front of my sister.

"Please remove your arm from your sleeve," I instructed.

Using an alcohol wipe, I cleaned the side of her shoulder and bicep, then blew on her skin to help it dry faster. After prepping the site, I taped the picture I had designated for my sister to her arm and began tracing over the lines with my markers. Slowly, the colors bled through the paper and onto her skin. I removed the barrier and filled in the rest of the design.

When my work was complete, I capped the marker and stepped back. "You've been given the wolf," I announced. "This is because you are a fierce protector and leader of your pack."

Loretta smiled. I knew she'd like the sounds of that.

I moved to Louie next, before he changed his mind.

Following the same procedure, I gave him a turtle. "The turtle will keep you protected," I explained.

Louie sighed in relief. If there was anything he wanted right then, it was to be kept safe. "Thank you," he said.

I handed Loretta the last picture and pulled off my hoodie. My sister cleaned my shoulder and attached the paper to my skin, same as I'd done to her. Then she took my marker and began tracing the lines.

"Okay, I think I'm done," she said after a few minutes.

I looked down at my tattoo and nodded. "You've given me the bear track."

"What does that mean?" Louie asked.

"The bear will bring us good luck," I declared.

Louie grinned. "Oh, that's a good one."

Loretta laughed. "What's next?" she asked.

"We should burn something in the fire, as a gift to the Forest Spirits," I said. "And then we dance."

"You aren't suggesting we burn something alive like they do in the movies, are you?!" she questioned, becoming alarmed for the first time all night.

"No," I scoffed. "Nothing like that."

Louie sighed. "Thank goodness," he mumbled.

"We can throw our scraps and wrappers in," I said. "That will suffice."

We tossed our papers into the pit, and the fire sprang to life, excited by the new fuel.

"Now dance," I encouraged, shuffling and bending my way around the circle to show them what I meant.

Loretta and Louie joined in, slow at first, but soon the Forest Spirits overcame us and we put on a wild and crazy performance. My ponytail whipped back and forth as we bobbed and weaved in the firelight.

Our routine probably looked more like a clown show than a dance, but it was the thought that mattered. We continued moving and laughing until the flames fell low; then we came to a stop. The three of us stood outside the fire, our tattoos and faces highlighted by the glow of burning embers, soaking in the strength and presence of the Forest Spirits.

Louie reached for his inhaler and took a puff.

"You use that a lot," I pointed out.

"Yeah, more than I should, probably," he acknowledged. "It's a nervous habit. I need to get back home now."

Loretta glanced at me, and I nodded.

"Round up your gear, soldiers," she commanded, taking charge again. "It's time to move out."

20

LORETTA

Returning Louie

I didn't have a formal plan going to the fortress, so I let Waylon do his fire ceremony. It was fine, maybe even a little fun. I'll admit, I wasn't too sure when he started talking about tattoos, but I couldn't chicken out. That wouldn't be setting a good example. Besides, maybe giving Waylon the chance to be our leader was another way of preparing him to be on his own—to take care of himself, as Dad would say. Maybe this summer wasn't just about building muscles but also finding a voice.

Ha! Who was I kidding? The boy needed muscles. At least the dance was physical and had us sweating by the end, so that had to count for something, but I definitely needed to get back to Mr. Miyagi ASAP.

Waylon did a triple check on the fire to make sure it was dead, and then we moved out. I could see how pleased and proud my brother was leaving our camp that night. According to him, the Forest Spirits would be with us from henceforth. I never imagined that there'd come a time when I'd be so thankful for that.

"Okay," I said, pausing to catch my breath when we reached the edge of the woods behind Louie's house. "We'll meet again tomorrow."

"I don't know if I'll be able to make it," Louie confessed. "It'll depend."

"Depend on what?" Waylon asked. "If your mom is asleep?"

"Yeah," Louie mumbled, staring at the ground.

"Why does she sleep during the day?" Waylon asked, eager to know more about the woman we'd seen inside Mimi's.

"She just does sometimes."

"What about your dad?" Waylon asked next, not slowing down.

"Look, I'll be there if I can make it," Louie snapped, putting an end to the questions.

I'd had enough chats with my father to know a thing or two about evasive answers. Louie wasn't ready to tell us more—not yet.

"We'll be waiting for you at the fortress," I said.

Louie nodded. Then the three of us crept forward, leaving the cover of the forest, and streaked across the backyard up to his house. Waylon and I held Dad's ladder, and Louie made the climb.

Once he was inside, Waylon and I raced back to the safety of the forest. We brought Dad's ladder with us this time and stashed it in the underbrush, hoping he wouldn't go looking for it anytime soon. We couldn't remember the last time he'd used it, so we were counting on that fact to mean he wouldn't notice. Also, we'd be needing it again.

Dad had explained the adolescent brain to me on numerous occasions during our chats. The frontal lobe of mine wasn't fully developed yet, which was the reason young kids like me tended to be risk-takers. What can I say? Our first sneak-out mission had been a thrilling success, so of course I wanted to do it again. Could you blame me?

21

LORETTA

Dad's Onto Us

Waylon and I did a good job of playing everything normal at breakfast the next morning. My brother had his face behind a book, and I was still rubbing the sleep from my eyes when I sat down at the table.

It was Saturday, so Mom was at the gym for her spin class. Dad was busy preparing our food—and singing, of course. Waylon glanced at me and smirked when Dad started bellowing to Johnny Cash's tune "Ring of Fire." *If he only knew,* I thought, and grinned. Turns out, he did!

Dad unplugged the griddle and joined us at the table with a tower of pancakes and the syrup. He always did the cooking and getting things ready, and then Waylon and I took care of the cleanup.

"Thanks," Waylon and I said, digging in. (Late-night adventures make you hungry.)

"Thought you might be starving," Dad said, sipping his coffee.

That was an odd comment, but he didn't say anything

more, so I left it alone. We ate our pancakes and made small talk, and I decided I was just being paranoid—until Dad made another sly remark.

"So do you have plans for the woods again today?" he asked.

Waylon and I looked at each other, then shrugged.

"I spent quite a bit of time out there with your uncle Rusty when I was a kid."

I stopped chewing. Dad didn't mention his brother that often, but I knew Uncle Rusty was his hero growing up. And that he was a lot of fun but lacked direction in life, so when he turned twenty, he enlisted in the service. That had been a good decision until he didn't make it back home. Mom had told me there was a lot Dad didn't understand about his daredevil brother, which was one of the reasons he was drawn to study the brain and people's behaviors.

"I've got some good memories of your uncle and me exploring those woods and building forts—and even sneaking out once or twice to spend the night at our hangout," Dad mused, "but don't tell your mother I told you that."

Waylon glanced at me, and I gave my head a subtle shake. How much did Dad know? The answer was I had no idea, so I wasn't about to let my brother say anything that might incriminate us. We continued eating and stayed quiet until Dad finished reminiscing and came back to real time.

"Well, I'm glad my coffee smells good because you two do not," he said, lowering his cup.

I almost choked on my pancake. Did we reek of campfire? I wasn't wearing my same clothes from last night, but Waylon still had his same T-shirt on. Gross boy! Wasn't it enough that I was trying to toughen him up, now I had to teach him about hygiene too?!

"You'd best make showering part of your days, and I suggest you do it before Mom gets home and starts asking questions."

That was enough warning for us. Waylon and I stuffed the last bits of pancake into our mouths and practically jumped from the table. We put our plates in the dishwasher and hurried to our bedrooms.

"Have fun today," Dad said as we were leaving. "And don't do anything I wouldn't do."

Whatever that was supposed to mean. I'd gone from thinking *if he only knew* to *how much did he know?*

"Okay," I said to Waylon when we reached our bedrooms. "We need to be more careful. I can't believe you wore those same clothes to breakfast, but what's done is done. Let's get showered and out of here before Mom returns."

Waylon nodded.

"You can go first," I said. "Dad was right. You stink."

Waylon made a face, then sniffed his armpit to see if I was telling the truth. I about gagged. Boys were disgusting.

I went into my bedroom and left my brother wallowing in his own stench.

*   *   *

A short while later, we were clean and on our way to the fortress. We'd managed to get away before Mom got back home, so we left her a note. Dad was busy tinkering with his lawn mower. The repair shop was booked solid for the next five weeks, so he was trying to fix it himself. He was too stubborn to buy a new one. Mom let him have his way, but in the meantime, she hired a landscape company to take care of the yard. As she'd told Dad, there were probably ten or more companies just in our small town to choose from and she was picking one. The crew had mowed once already when Waylon and I were at camp and things looked great—even Dad had to admit that, although begrudgingly. Needless to say, sneaking past him and his mower was easy.

You know what else was easy? Traveling through the forest in daylight compared to the pitch-black. It was way less scary too. I didn't mention any of that to Waylon because I was supposed to be the wolf, but I sure thought it.

Dad had surprised us at breakfast, but an even bigger surprise awaited us at the fortress. Louie was already there. He sat on the Circle of Stones, drinking from his canteen.

"You made it!" Waylon exclaimed.

Louie lowered his water and swallowed. "A soldier never backs out of a mission, especially when he has the turtle," he said, patting his shoulder.

Waylon grinned.

"Your mother's asleep again?" I said.

He nodded.

"But what if she wakes up while you're out?" Waylon asked.

"She took her sleeping pills, so she won't. I have at least three hours," Louie replied.

Sleeping pills, I thought. *Must be what she gets at the pharmacy. And they sure knock her out.*

"What about your father?" Waylon asked next.

"You don't have to worry about him."

Boy, did I have questions after that evasive answer, but I didn't push it. When Dad talked about his job, he always said it was important to give a person time, to let them open up on their own terms. His role was to give the person a safe space to talk when they were ready— and to listen. I was listening, and what I was hearing was Louie telling us he wasn't ready yet.

"Great," Waylon said, interrupting my thoughts. "What's our plan, then?" he asked, eager to get started.

That was the question. Trouble was, I didn't know the answer. Maybe trying to be Mr. Miyagi was the wrong approach? I needed to channel the Force.

"To the Millennium Falcon," I declared.

"The Millennium Falcon?" Louie repeated.

"You'll see," Waylon assured him. "C'mon."

22

LORETTA

Treasure!

"Wow! This is awesome!" Louie exclaimed the moment he saw the Millennium Falcon. "It's our own army tank. Man your battle stations!" he yelled.

So much for Star Wars, I thought.

Louie flung his backpack aside and climbed to the topmost part. Waylon and I watched with big grins. What we neglected to do was tell Louie to be careful, and before we could warn him, he jumped from his high post to the lower platform. When he landed, his right leg punched through the rusty metal all the way up to his thigh.

"Whoa!" Waylon shouted. "Are you okay?"

We rushed to Louie's side.

"I think so. I feel something funny under my foot. Help me get out of this hole so we can see what it is."

Together, Waylon and I grabbed Louie under his armpits. "On three," Waylon said. "One. Two. Three."

We yanked up as hard as we could and barely managed to get Louie's knee back above the hole, but that was enough. From there he was able to sit and free himself the rest of the way.

"You're lucky you didn't get hurt," I said.

"He's got the turtle. Forest Spirits were protecting him," Waylon reminded us, as if that was fact.

Louie grinned. "Yeah, I've got the turtle," he repeated, patting his shoulder.

"Let's see what you felt under your foot," Waylon said.

"Yeah," I agreed. I hurried and crawled over to the hole and peered down before my brother could—just so he couldn't. Brothers and sisters do that sort of thing to each other.

"It looks like there's some sort of box down there," I described. "I can just see the shape of it. There's one edge sticking up. I think that's what you—"

"Lemme see!" Waylon yelled.

"It's not that big. About the size of a box of chocolates—"

"Lemme see!" Waylon yelled again.

"There's some sort of cloth wrapped around it," I continued, ignoring his pleas.

"That's it! Look out!" Waylon yelled, shoving me out of the way after I'd teased him enough. He stuck his head above the hole. "That's no box of chocolates!" he cried. "That's buried treasure!"

"Hooah!" Louie cheered.

Waylon got up. "The bear tracks have brought us good luck," he exclaimed. "We're gonna be rich!"

Unable to contain his excitement, my brother jumped to the ground and got down on his belly. He was the smallest among us, so it made sense for him to be the one to army crawl his way underneath the combine. Trust me, I wasn't looking to do that. Besides, grunt work had to count for some sort of training.

Louie and I watched from above as Waylon slithered and squirmed his way across the ground. Once he was fully underneath the Falcon, he had more room and was able to crawl on his hands and knees. He moved quickly to the treasure and brushed the dirt off the top.

"Don't open it," I yelled. "We need to bring it back to the fortress and go through it together."

"You're right," he agreed, surprising me. "We need to hold a fire ceremony to cast away any demons that might be inside before opening it."

"What're we, pirates now?" I scoffed.

"Don't mess around with the spirits," he warned, dead serious.

His response reminded me of Indiana Jones and Aladdin. Both touch the forbidden treasure, which then sets off a slew of deadly booby traps. Waylon was right. I wasn't messing around.

Louie had something else on his mind. "Do you mean we're gonna sneak out again tonight?" he asked.

I didn't get the chance to respond because just then Waylon went ahead and lifted the box out of the ground, and as soon as he did, a long black snake slithered out from underneath it—my brother's kryptonite.

"Ahhh!" he screamed, and I mean *sc-reeeamed*. What came out of Waylon rivaled that scene in *Home Alone* when Kevin plops Buzz's tarantula on the bad guy's face. Ever see it? You need to. That is the greatest scream of all movie screams—and my brother had just matched it! In his panic, Waylon dropped the box and jumped to his feet, forgetting he didn't have room for that. His head collided with the underside of the combine floor.

"Oww!" he yelped, falling back to his knees and rubbing at his injury. Like any good sister, I found it hysterical. I was laughing my butt off—until Waylon pulled his hands away, and I saw all the blood.

"Oh my God! Waylon! Are you okay?" I cried.

He didn't answer. The color in his face vanished.

"He's going into shock," Louie said. "He's gonna faint."

On cue, Waylon began swaying, then fell to the ground like a wet blanket.

"Waylon!" I screamed.

"We need to get to him," Louie said. "Watch out."

I slid aside, feeling numb. I think I was the one going into shock now.

With his good leg, Louie kicked at the sides of the hole. I didn't know if he'd always had that power harnessed in his body, or if it was from the adrenaline rush, but two hard blows and he'd bent the metal back so that the hole was suddenly large enough for us to fit through. Louie dropped to the ground, and I followed behind him.

"Waylon," Louie said, gently shaking my brother's limp body. "Waylon," he said again.

I held my breath. After several long seconds, Waylon moaned. His eyelids began to flicker.

"He's waking up!" I cheered with relief.

"Where's the snake?" Waylon mumbled.

Louie chuckled. "It's gone. It left while you were dancing around down here."

Waylon gave a weak laugh.

Louie put his hand behind Waylon's back and helped him sit up. He held him there for a minute to make sure Waylon wasn't going to fall flat again; then he began inspecting Waylon's injury. "The one thing about head cuts is that they can bleed like crazy, even little scrapes like this one," he said.

"You mean it's not bad?" I asked.

"No. It's hardly anything, but let me take care of it."

Louie grabbed his pack from above the hole. He unzipped it and pulled out a first-aid kit. Not your everyday, over-the-counter wimpy thing, but a real-deal medical kit, also army-looking, like everything else about him.

I watched Louie clean Waylon's wound and add ointment to the area. "I can't put a bandage on it because your hair is in the way, so keep this gauze pressed against the spot for now," he instructed.

"Thanks," Waylon said.

"You're lucky it didn't need stitches. I could've tried doing those, but it wouldn't have been fun for you."

"You know how to do stitches?" I was impressed.

"The proper term is sutures, and sort of. I've practiced on fake skin, but I've never done them on a real person."

"Where did you learn to do that?"

Louie hesitated, then said, "My father."

"Is that where you got that med kit too?" I asked next, seizing my opening.

He nodded. "C'mon, let's get our treasure back to the fortress." He was done with my line of questioning.

Louie gave Waylon a boost through the hole. I climbed up and out next. Louie followed.

Waylon's small medical emergency had brought something out in Louie and had me wondering more about his army obsession and medical talents, but it was time for me to take charge again. Answers would come later.

"Okay, let's move out," I commanded.

23

WAYLON

Opening the Treasure

My head was sore, but I wasn't letting that slow me down. I kept the gauze pressed against my cut, and after Loretta's command to move out, I took the lead and got us back to the fortress as fast as possible. Louie and Loretta plopped down around the Circle of Stones, drinking from their waters. Not me. I couldn't wait to see what treasure awaited us—but first things first.

"As much as I would like to unwrap the box and rip it open," I admitted, "we can't do that or—"

"I don't have time for a fire ceremony," Louie interrupted, closing his canteen, "but I have a different idea that I think the Forest Spirits will appreciate."

I glanced at my sister, who shrugged. "What?" we asked him.

Louie dug into his backpack again, except this time, instead of retrieving medical supplies, he pulled out a harmonica. "How about a music ceremony?" he said, bringing the small instrument to his lips. As soon as he began playing, a gentle breeze blew through the area and then everything around us seemed to fall silent. Louie had the spirits and all the forest's creatures listening. He filled the air with a beautiful melody before finishing on a soft low note.

"Where did you learn to play like that?" Loretta asked.

"I started playing before I could even talk. I'm not named after my great-grandpa, but my dad did name me after Louis Armstrong, one of the greatest trumpet players of all time."

"It could be worse," Loretta groaned. "Your father could've named you after a famous country music singer like mine did."

Louie grinned. "I wondered, but I wasn't saying anything after you almost beat me up."

Loretta laughed. "Anything else you're wondering?"

"Actually, yeah. Are you really twins?"

"Fraternal twins," I answered. "I got the good looks, and Loretta got the attitude."

Louie laughed at my joke while Loretta sneered.

"And one more thing," Louie said, growing too confident. "Is that your blankie I've seen you carrying in your backpack?"

"Careful, Captain Camo," Loretta warned. "Watch your step."

"So can you play the trumpet?" I asked Louie, steering him away from trouble.

"Yeah, that's my main instrument," he said, "but carrying that out here would be kinda hard."

"Well, the harmonica was awesome," I told him. "The spirits are sure to have loved it."

"Thanks."

I checked my gauze and was relieved to see I'd stopped bleeding. It was time to get down to business. "We can now proceed with the opening ceremony," I declared.

"As the wolf, I should be the one to lead the opening," Loretta proclaimed, putting her hand on the box.

I could've argued that as the finder it was Louie's job to open it, but I didn't want to prolong the suspense any longer. I was ready to see what was inside.

Loretta placed the box on the ground in front of us. She removed the twine holding the cloth in place and unwrapped the covering, giving us our first glimpse of the old wooden cigar box. Louie and I skooched forward. We knelt side by side, barely breathing. This was the moment.

Loretta turned the box so that the front was facing her. She flipped the small latch holding it closed and slowly lifted the top. Ever so carefully, she leaned over and peeked inside.

"Ahhh!" she screamed, slamming it shut.

Naturally, Louie and I screamed too. Actually, we grabbed each other in a hug. My not-so-funny sister burst into a fit of uncontrollable laughter.

Realizing the joke was on us, Louie and I brushed ourselves off.

"Real funny. Now open it," I growled, out of patience. Even if the Forest Spirits were amused, I was not.

The last thing Louie wanted was to get caught in the middle of a brother-sister squabble, so he kept his mouth shut.

Loretta wiped her tears and managed to gain control and refocus. Once again, she gripped the box and lifted the top.

This time Louie and I sprang forward to see what was inside and smacked heads in a wicked collision. We fell over groaning and holding fresh goose eggs. Forget the gauze, now I needed an ice pack. Loretta got another good laugh and then began sifting through the contents without us.

"There's nothing here," she groaned, shoving the box in disgust. "I should've never listened to you and your stupid ideas about a treasure."

Louie and I sat up and pulled the box closer. It was true; there wasn't much in it. I found a lighter, a small Buzz Lightyear action figure, an orange rabbit's foot, and a cassette tape (at least, I think that's what it was called). I picked up each object and inspected them one by one. Louie lifted a yellowed magazine off the bottom.

"Whoa," he whispered.

He closed it and handed it to me without saying anything more. Whoa, was right. This wasn't just any old magazine. It was a dirty magazine. My eyes popped.

"Give me that!" Loretta snapped when she realized what I had.

"No way! You're not our mother, and besides, you had your chance. You said there was nothing in there."

"That's something P.E. Bubba would have," she shrieked. "Give it to me."

She lunged for the magazine, but I was too quick. I yanked it out of her reach.

Now she was angry. "Look at that," I said to Louie, egging her on. I hadn't actually seen anything.

Loretta lunged again, this time with extra aggression. She connected with my arm and sent the magazine flying through the air. A small piece of paper fell from its fluttering pages. The paper flipped, swooped, and gently floated to the ground in front of us.

It was a piece of paper that would change our lives forever.

24

LORETTA

The Note

I picked up the paper and read it aloud.

"Dear Seeker, the purpose of this box is twofold: First, it serves as a time capsule. Inside are several sentimental artifacts, sacrificed in the interest of storytelling . . . in case I don't make it home."

I swallowed, then glanced at my brother and Louie.

"Is there more?" Louie asked, taking a puff from his inhaler.

I nodded, then looked down and continued. *"Second, this box presents your quest. I challenge you to make similar sacrifices, and I dare you to find and conquer your own rite of passage, as I prepare to face my own. In doing so, may we find ourselves."*

I glanced at my brother and Louie a second time before reading the last line. They were hanging on to every word. I took a deep breath. *"And know this,"* I read. *"Whether I'm here or someplace else, I'll always be with you. Ron."*

Dear Seeker:

The purpose of this box is twofold:
First, it serves as a time capsule. Inside are several sentimental artifacts, sacrificed in the interest of history and storytelling—in case I don't make it home.
Second, this box presents your quest. I challenge you to make similar sacrifices, and I dare you to find and conquer your own rite of passage, as I prepare to face my own. In doing so, may we find ourselves.
And know this. Whether I'm here or someplace else, I'll always be with you.

RON

I lowered the paper and slowly let the air out of my lungs. The three of us sat in silence, feeling the weight of the words I'd just read.

"So these are sentimental artifacts," Louie mused, turning Buzz Lightyear over in his hand.

"That's what the note says," I replied. "There's a story behind every item in there."

"Wish we knew the stories," he said, "and who Ron was."

"Yeah, but that's not what's important," Waylon

responded. "The Forest Spirits have spoken. We've been given a quest."

"I don't know," Louie worried, shaking his head.

"We must accept the challenge," Waylon implored. "Otherwise we risk disappointing the spirits—and ourselves."

"Waylon's right," I agreed. "We can do this." I certainly didn't know what I was getting myself into, but the way I saw it, here was my chance for more Mr. Miyagi. I couldn't afford to pass it up.

Waylon's chest swelled. With me on his side, he knew it was happening.

Louie's shoulders sagged. "So what's next?" he asked, giving in.

"A second fire ceremony," Waylon answered. "A ceremony of sacrifices. We must come prepared to make ours."

"When you say sacrifices . . . you don't plan on killing something . . . do you?" Louie asked hesitantly.

"No!" I shouted, not even giving my brother the chance to consider that. "Absolutely not!" I emphasized. "That sort of stuff is only for the movies. We're not in *King Kong* or *Indiana Jones*. The note says we must sacrifice something personally sentimental. That's all."

"Phew," Louie replied, wiping his brow and taking another puff from his inhaler.

"We should wait a few days before holding the ceremony," Waylon suggested. "If we disappear again tomorrow, Mom's liable to start asking questions, and we've already got Dad to worry about. Plus, we need time to plan our sacrifices."

"You're right," I agreed.

I turned to Louie. "We'll give it until Friday, and then we'll be at your house at midnight."

He took a deep breath. "Okay," he conceded. "Just be careful. My mom can't catch us or—"

"Else," I finished. "Or else. I know."

"Yeah, or else," he repeated.

Waylon left the fortress with unwavering conviction and excitement that afternoon.

Louie, on the other hand, left worried on top of scared. Two puffs from his inhaler didn't help that.

I left with a dirty magazine in my pack. I refused to let those two have another look at that smut.

25

LORETTA

New Developments

Sacrifices and dares and rites of passage. It all sounded crazy—even dangerous. But my scrawny brother—who I thought wasn't tough—was brave and determined if he was anything at all, so he wasn't backing down. He was ready to take the challenge and discover what lay ahead. In fact, he wouldn't stop talking about it.

"Have you decided what you'll be sacrificing yet?" he asked me Sunday night. He didn't want me to tell him what because he said it needed to be a surprise, something between me and the Forest Spirits. He only wanted to know if I'd reached a decision.

"No," I answered.

"Have you decided what you'll be sacrificing yet?" he asked me again on Monday morning.

"No," I answered again.

"Have you decided what you'll be sacrificing yet?" he asked me (for the hundredth time) on Monday night.

"No," I answered (for the hundredth time). "Why are you so excited to get rid of something anyway?"

"Loretta, this is a pivotal moment in our lives. This isn't about fun. It's about finding out who we are. I'm scared more than anything else."

Up till then, I'd been thinking of sacrificing an old hair scrunchie or magazine of my own. Tell you the truth, other than when Waylon pestered me about it, I hadn't given it much thought. But once Waylon told me he was scared, I realized this was far more serious.

The good news: I still had time to prepare before the special fire ceremony. The bad news: I had to return to camp before that. If there was a way for me to sacrifice P.E. Bubba to the fire, trust me, I would've—especially after he messed with Waylon.

Being camp director meant P.E. got to do next to nothing while his hired counselors took care of running the show. He did what he had to on the first day, but since then, he got his kicks out of driving around with the top down in his fancy sports car, going from location to location to check on the various groups, making it seem like he was actually doing something when he wasn't.

These were pertinent details for what ultimately happened, but before I get ahead of myself with car stories, I need to mention some other developments. First off, camp wasn't all bad. Now that P.E. had assumed the role of driving around, I wasn't stuck looking at his face—or belly. All I had to do was play sports—and I actually enjoyed that. And since Waylon was tucked away with his robot peeps in a safe place across the road, I didn't need to worry about him—or so I thought.

Our counselors gave us the choice between participating in basketball or soccer. I went with soccer because even though I didn't have a lot of experience, I was fast. As fast or faster than anyone else on the field, even in my bald sneakers on the wet grass—and it was wet! It had rained buckets overnight.

My socks and sneakers were soaked by the end of our game and I hate wet socks, but even so, I had fun. I scored three goals and high-fived two girls whose names I didn't even know. (I later learned they were Grace and Alyssa.) Like I said, camp wasn't that bad—until we returned to the youth center and I spotted Waylon standing on the other side of the road, getting ready to cross so that he could join the rest of us waiting for our rides. But before he did, there was a girl, equal in his height, who called his name from behind. Waylon turned and smiled when he saw her. What he didn't see was the fancy sports car approaching. P.E. veered into a big puddle as he neared my brother, sending a wave of water into the air that drenched Waylon from head to toe.

The girl, whoever she was, came running. When she caught up to him, Waylon just looked at her and shrugged. Then they laughed. Laughed! She never even seemed to apologize for distracting him. That was it. I didn't trust her. Had she seen P.E. coming and tricked my brother?

I can tell you this: I wasn't laughing, especially when P.E. came waltzing from his car with that stupid grin on his face, acting like he didn't know what had just happened. What was my rule? Don't mess with my brother. P.E. Bubba was gonna get what was coming to him—and this time it was going to be worse than a penalty kick.

But he wasn't the only thing that irked me. Waylon was still standing with that girl—even though he'd crossed to my side of the road now. Who did she think she was? She'd better watch her step or she was gonna be answering to me.

26

WAYLON

Disappearing on Loretta

I made sure to get to breakfast before my sister on Wednesday morning so that I could fill Dad in on my plan. I didn't like tricking Loretta, but that was the only way I was going to get away without her following me or trying to tag along. Dad was okay with me going to the library because this was part of us showing my sister that I was capable on my own—and also because I didn't tell him everything. It wasn't that I was worried he'd object, but if Dad knew I was meeting up with a girl, then he'd have questions—lots of them.

Penelope asked me if I wanted to meet up at the library after our robotics teacher recommended that we play chess and other strategy games if we were serious about computers and programming. Stevens Library had a beautiful chess set and table for their patrons to use. I liked chess, but I also liked hanging out with Penelope. She had gone to a different elementary school in town, so we'd never been together before. She was super smart and super cool, and I was already excited about attending middle school with her—but I had to be careful.

Loretta had grilled me about "that girl" after she'd seen Penelope and me hanging out together after camp. "Who is she? Did she see P.E. coming and trick you so that you'd get splashed?"

"Her name is Penelope, and no, she didn't trick me," I said. "She doesn't like P.E. any more than you do. She made a joke about the sun gleaming off his bald head, which was why we were laughing. You need to relax."

"I don't trust her. You need to be careful."

I didn't say anything more, but I heeded Loretta's advice. I was being careful—around her! I waited until my sister got engrossed in one of her movies, and then I made my getaway.

Penelope was waiting for me when I rolled up to the bike rack outside the library. We parked side by side and went into the building. The chess table was open, so we got to sit down right away—which was a relief because I couldn't disappear on Loretta for too long.

"White goes first," Penelope said.

I glanced over my shoulder, making sure I wasn't followed, then settled in. "Who taught you to play?" I asked her after making my move.

"My dad. And you?" She slid her pawn forward.

"Same. Though my mom is probably a better player."

Penelope smiled. "What do your parents do?"

I told her about Dad being a psychologist and Mom a vet while analyzing the board.

"Really? I love animals," Penelope gushed. "Animals

aren't judgmental like people. My dog, Chief, loves me no matter what."

"Chief?" I mused. "Is Chief a big dog?" I pushed my castle ahead.

"No," she giggled. "He's—"

"A little guy with a big name," I said before she could finish.

"Exactly. How'd you guess?"

"And he screams when he gets his shots?" I added.

"Yes," she said. "How'd you know that?"

"My mom is Dr. Neal, your vet. She told us all about Chief. She really likes your dog."

"Chief really likes her," Penelope said. "And so do I."

"Yeah, she's okay," I replied.

Penelope laughed. Then she moved her knight to the right two spaces and back one. "Check."

Check? Already? Whoa! I studied the board, then looked up and returned her smile. She was good. I moved out of danger and asked about her parents next.

I needed to pay better attention before she had me trapped, but that wasn't happening. I heard something behind me and spun around, scared that it could be Loretta showing up unannounced. Had she tracked me down?

I exhaled when I saw that it was just the librarian reshelving books, but that was enough to put me on edge. Whenever it wasn't my turn, I was glancing around the room. Loretta never appeared, but I didn't push it. After two games—Penelope won both—I decided to get going.

First, though, I asked Penelope to make a pit stop with

me at the nonfiction area of the library so that I could find a book about sacrifices.

"Interesting" was her remark when she saw what I'd selected.

"Research," I replied, and left it at that.

The truth was I needed an alibi ready for Loretta, a way to explain why I'd disappeared on her. When I showed her the book and mentioned something about human sacrifices, she'd freak out and forget all about me ditching her—I hoped.

After checking out my book, Penelope and I exited the library and grabbed our bikes from the rack. I stashed the book in the basket attached to my front handlebars and was clipping the strap on my helmet when she started waving to someone behind me.

I whipped around, thinking it was Loretta. But Penelope didn't know my sister. I hadn't pointed her out at camp. I was being paranoid. Unfortunately, that wasn't a relief because seeing who Penelope *was* waving to made me even jumpier.

Standing across the road, leaf blower in hand, was Leon Hurd. What happened next was an involuntary reflex. I waved. And then I immediately looked away after realizing what a terrible mistake I'd just committed.

"You know him?" I croaked.

"Leon and his brother mow our lawn," Penelope explained.

I gulped. "He's a mean kid."

"He's always friendly to me," she said, sticking up for him.

"Yeah, well, he's not nice in school," I countered.

"My dad told me life hasn't been easy for him. His mom left when he was little."

That was sad. Maybe there was more to Leon Hurd than any of us knew, but I still wasn't so sure "friendly" was a word I'd ever use to describe him. "Well, guess I'll see you at camp," I said, climbing on my bike.

"See you," she said.

As I pedaled down the sidewalk, I glanced in Leon Hurd's direction. He saw me and held my gaze. I pushed my pedals a lot harder.

Next up, my sister. Talking to Leon Hurd would've been less scary.

27

WAYLON

Explaining to Loretta

Loretta was waiting for me in the garage when I got home. She stood with her arms folded and feet planted, scowling. Forget the wolf—she was a king cobra, hood flared, ready to strike. As you know, I'm not good with snakes.

"Since when do we ditch each other?" she hissed, coming at me before I'd even parked my bike.

I climbed off my seat and put the kickstand down. "You were watching a movie, and I didn't want to bother you. It was only a quick trip."

"I don't call three hours a quick trip. What if you'd run into Leon Hurd? That kid has been around every turn, stalking us."

I thought about telling her but stopped short. If she knew that I'd seen him and escaped unharmed, she might consider it luck and see my near-death experience as proof that I shouldn't go anywhere without her, that I needed her by my side at all times, and the goal was to show her the exact opposite.

"I'm sorry," I said. "I didn't mean to be gone so long. I started reading and lost track of the time."

She eyed the book I had in my basket.

I picked it up. "Don't freak out," I said, "but it's a look at the history of sacrifices. From crazy scary stuff like human offerings back in the 1400s and earlier, to animal sacrifices, to more recent stuff."

"Jeez, Waylon. Now you're scaring me. What exactly do you have planned?"

"Nothing like that, so relax. We've been challenged to part with sentimental artifacts, like Andy did at the end of *Toy Story 3*. Remember when he gave Buzz and Woody and the rest of the gang to that little girl Bonnie?"

"That part made me cry."

"I know. Our sacrifices need to mean something like that. Think of what we found in the cigar box. We don't know the stories behind those pieces, but they meant something. Letting go wasn't easy."

Loretta's face, her body language, everything about her changed as she began to grapple with what I was saying. Gone was the king cobra. "You'll be ready," I assured her. "I know you will. You're the wolf."

I walked inside then and left my sister standing in the garage, pondering her future. Tricking her into forgetting about my disappearance and putting the king cobra back to sleep was easier than I'd expected, but what lay ahead was going to be far harder—for all of us.

28

LORETTA

Getting Real

Camp on Thursday was a hot mess. No, there wasn't any trouble with P.E. Bubba. Yes, I still owed him—I wasn't about to forget that—but P.E. would need to wait because there was something more pressing in my life—Waylon's expectations for our upcoming ceremony of sacrifices. I doubted my favorite scrunchie was going to be worthy enough.

With my mind swirling, I went from being an all-star soccer player to all-around pathetic. It was so bad that Alyssa—or maybe it was Grace, I couldn't keep them straight—actually asked me, "Are you feeling all right?"

I told her the truth. "Not really."

"I didn't think so. You should take it easy. Alyssa and I will pick up the slack."

Guess she was Grace. "Thanks," I said.

As suggested, I took it easy for the rest of soccer, but that only helped for so long. I felt worse when I saw Waylon walking and laughing with that girl again on his way back from robotics. And then a thought came to me. What if my brother had ditched me to go and see her yesterday? *No, he wouldn't,* I told myself.

Fortunately, I didn't have to stomach watching them for long because the girl's ride was waiting and she left as soon as they got back to the youth center. Waylon came and found me after she was gone.

"Is she your girlfriend?" I said, a bit nastier than I'd meant.

"Who?" he replied, playing dumb. I'd seen too many movies to fall for that.

"That girl," I said.

"Penelope?" he scoffed. "No! We just hang out at robotics."

My eyes narrowed.

"Have you decided on your sacrifice yet?"

I didn't answer. He was trying to change the subject. I wasn't falling for that either.

"I have," he said.

"Oh, yeah?"

"Yeah," he replied. "The ceremony is tomorrow night, Loretta."

I shrugged.

"You know what I think?"

"What?"

"I think you know what you need to sacrifice and you're scared."

"Pfft. No, I'm not."

"I'm scared," Waylon admitted. "If you're not, then I'm not sure you've selected the right object."

Dad pulled up then, and that was the end of our conversation. We didn't talk about it anymore until the time finally came.

It was just after midnight on Friday when Waylon and I crouched in the underbrush surveying Louie's house.

"Looks quiet," Waylon said. "Let's go."

"You're too late," a voice behind us whispered, simultaneously clamping a hand over each of our mouths and stifling our screams. My heart pounded against my chest. Gradually, the person's grip eased, and Waylon and I spun around.

"Now we're even," Louie said, and grinned.

I punched him in the chest. "Not funny," I hissed. "It's already spooky enough out here without you pulling a stunt like that. What would you have done if our screams escaped?"

Waylon smirked and shrugged. "You got us."

I wasn't in the mood. "Let's go," I growled. "We've got a big night ahead of us. Any more fooling around and I'll knock your heads together."

That did the trick. They knew I wasn't joking. Waylon took the lead and we double-timed it to the fortress and dropped our packs around the Circle of Stones, but we didn't rest for long. After a couple of puffs from his inhaler, and quick drinks for both of us, Louie and I began gathering wood and kindling so Waylon could build our fire.

"Waylon, here," I said when it appeared he had things

close to ready. I held out Ron's lighter, the one we'd found inside the box. "It only seems right that we use this as we begin our quest."

"Good call," he agreed. "This will help connect us with the spirits."

"How do you suppose the lighter became an object worthy of sacrifice?" Louie asked, surprising us with his question. He was still wondering about the stories behind the pieces.

I shrugged. "I don't know. Maybe it was used to light candles on a memorable occasion. Or a first cigarette," I offered as possibilities.

"Or maybe it belonged to somebody else before," Louie said, "somebody special, and the lighter was all they had left to remember that person by?"

My eyes narrowed. "What made you think of that?"

"When you sit around all day, you've got time to think of stuff like that, I guess."

"Is that what you do?" Waylon asked. "Just sit around?"

"I read. Watch TV. Play music. Get bored . . . Watch the clock as I wait for you guys."

I kinda felt sad for him after he said that.

"Well, you're not going to be bored tonight," Waylon promised. He flicked Ron's lighter, and a tiny flame danced to life. He held the flame under the kindling, and soon our fire began to grow.

My brother stood and faced us then. "It's time for our second fire ceremony—the Ceremony of Sacrifices," he announced.

I steadied myself, not wanting to give the impression I was nervous—but I'd been nervous all week. What did my brother have planned?

Waylon went to his backpack and started pulling out the now-familiar markers.

"We need more tattoos?" Louie asked.

"Yes," Waylon replied. "Tattoos are a vital part of every fire ceremony, and it's even more important before a sacrifice."

"I was afraid you'd say that."

"Didn't you like the turtle? And didn't it protect us?" Waylon said.

Louie grinned. "Yeah, it was cool," he admitted, rubbing his shoulder where the turtle was.

"You'll love tonight's, then," Waylon promised.

"Let's do it," Louie said, clapping his hands together and walking across the circle to where Waylon had his supplies set out. Whether Louie was only trying to pump himself up or if he was truly excited, I didn't know, but suddenly I was with two boys who'd found courage—and that just made me all the more anxious.

Using the same techniques, Waylon went to work on Louie's other shoulder. It didn't take him long, and then he stepped aside and made his proclamation. "Dr. Louie, I've given you the eye of the medicine man." He'd drawn two sideways diamonds, one inside the other, with a dot in the middle. "You're the healer, and you will keep us safe and in harmony with mother earth."

Louie straightened and puffed out his chest. Waylon had bestowed a great honor on him.

I went next. I didn't look at my shoulder until Waylon was finished. My new tattoo was pretty. The design was familiar, but I couldn't recall its name or what it meant.

"For our leader, I give you the dream catcher," Waylon said. "This will keep you connected with the spirits, who will bring you good visions and keep the bad ones away."

I liked the idea of keeping bad dreams away. *Sounds like something Louie's mother could use,* I thought.

"I'll do yours," Louie offered to my brother.

Waylon handed the paper to Louie and talked him through the procedure. Louie did a great job—he was better than me at tattooing—and he didn't stop there. Even though my brother had chosen the tattoo for himself, Louie was the one to make the proclamation.

"Waylon, you've been given the eagle, a majestic animal revered by the Forest Spirits. No matter what happens with our quests, may you continue to soar."

Waylon bowed his head, accepting the gift of the eagle, and then Louie began our dance. Waylon and I joined. We danced and danced, taking in the sounds and smells of the burning wood, feeling its heat.

When we slowed and came to a stop, I immediately took charge. I needed to see how serious Waylon planned on making this ordeal before I sacrificed anything.

"Tonight's challenge calls for us to make a sacrifice," I began. "Like those who've explored these woods before us, we will need to be strong. And brave."

Waylon remained calm, but I could see Louie's confidence beginning to waver. He'd been brave when it came to tattoos and dancing because he knew what to expect, but now we were entering unchartered waters.

"Captain Waylon, are you ready?" I asked.

Our night of fun and games was about to get very real.

29

LORETTA

Sacrifices

Waylon stepped forward. "Tonight's test is meant to pull at our emotions," he said. "We've been challenged to make a sentimental sacrifice. We must answer this challenge because only then will we be rewarded. We must let go of the past and face our futures."

My breathing quickened. Where was my brother going with this?

"Loretta, I need you to get my hatchet," he said, his voice low. "It's in my pack."

"I thought you said we weren't killing anything!" Louie cried. His voice was not low.

"We aren't," I assured him, fighting to steady my shaking hands. Taking slow and easy breaths, I summoned the courage to walk to Waylon's backpack. I returned with his hatchet, as requested. The firelight sparkled and reflected off its sleek silver blade.

"What are you going to do?" Louie begged. "No one gets cut or hurt," he said, trying to sound firm.

"Relax," Waylon commanded. "Your unraveling will upset the Forest Spirits. Trust them."

Louie took another zap from his inhaler but didn't say anything more. He stood by, wide-eyed and silent. I thought about asking him for a puff, but I doubted it would help. After what happened next, it wasn't an inhaler that I needed, but CPR.

Waylon stepped closer to the fire, absorbing its heat and energy. He draped his ponytail over his shoulder and held it while lifting his face to the sky. My brother's stoicism was impressive, especially because I now sensed what was coming—and I was too stunned to react.

I stayed back with Louie, watching my brother until his gaze returned to the fire and he nodded. That was my cue. I approached and stood beside him.

"Are you sure?" I whispered.

"It's time," he said, unblinking.

"You're really sure?" I asked again, fighting against the knot forming in my throat.

"Loretta, it's okay. Just do it."

I took a deep breath and let it out slowly. Then I moved behind my brother and grasped his ponytail in my left hand.

Louie gasped, suddenly understanding.

Squeezing the handle in my right fist, I brought the hatchet up. Then I gritted my teeth and pulled the silver blade across his hair. Waylon's tail fell. Five years dangled from my hand.

Waylon reached up and felt the back of his head, touching the area where his pony once hung. Slowly, he turned to me, and I handed him the rope of hair. Turning back to the fire, Waylon lifted his severed ponytail high above his head.

"Forest Spirits, I feel your presence. Please accept my sacrifice as a symbol of my faith. I'm ready to let go of the past and face the future."

And with those words, my brother tossed his once-prized possession into the fire. The eager flames sprang to life, energized by Waylon's gift. We watched in silence until the last of it was gone, and then we proceeded with the ceremony. I knew it was coming, but my heart still fluttered when Waylon asked me if I was ready.

I closed my eyes and took another deep breath, channeling the wolf. We had to be a pack, and I had to lead. One more deep breath, and then I looked at my brother and nodded. I walked over and knelt beside my backpack and unzipped it.

I reached inside and knocked my scrunchie out of the way, dug past my favorite T-shirt, and pushed aside my *Return of the Jedi* DVD—which I'd thought would be my ultimate sacrifice if Waylon got too serious, but even that was not enough. My throat tightened as my hand grasped the only worthy artifact.

I tore my favorite ragged corner off and stuck it inside my pocket next to the few strands of Waylon's pony that I'd also saved. I took a minute to myself, then stood and slowly approached the fire. Louie whimpered as I strode past. I kissed Blankie and lifted him up high.

"We remember, but we let go of the past and face our futures!" I shouted, my voice cracking. I sucked in a deep breath, and then I threw my beloved blanket into the fire. The hungry flames rose up and swallowed my faithful companion. I let go of my breath and watched as he was taken.

"Goodbye, Blankie," I whispered. "I promise I won't ever forget you." I wiped my face and turned around.

Like me, Louie's eyes were wet. I knew that was partly because of what he'd just witnessed, and partly because of what was to come. It was his turn. Two quick puffs from his inhaler; then he closed his eyes and took a deep breath, same as I had. One more breath and then he looked at Waylon and me and nodded, signaling he was ready.

We watched him reach into his pocket and pull out his harmonica, the same one he'd played so beautifully. The tarnished metal told me it was old, and the way Louie held it and gently rubbed his thumb across the top told me how much it meant to him. He approached the fire, cradling the instrument in his shaking hands.

Waylon and I never said a word. It would be a while before we learned the story behind the harmonica, but we could see—and feel.

Louie lifted the instrument to his lips, paused, and then he played. And I mean, *puh-laaayed*. A mesmerizing song poured from him, starting slow and building into a passionate middle, before slowing once more and finishing softly.

I had to wipe my face again.

Louie kissed the harmonica and whispered something to it. Then he tossed it into the fire.

Waylon and I stepped closer and stood beside him, watching the flames surround his gift. The metal turned shades of red and gold as it melted and warped under the heat.

"That was beautiful," I said.

Louie nodded and brushed his cheeks.

I reached over and took his hand in mine. I gripped Waylon's with my other. This wasn't anything I had planned, but it felt right. The three of us stood together, holding hands, staring into the orange glow, thinking about the pasts we'd let go of—and the futures we were yet to meet.

During that moment, I realized watching Louie and my brother make their sacrifices had been harder than making my own. I was beginning to understand the truly special bonds and forces that exist within a pack.

We stayed that way until the fire died down. When it was time, we covered the pit with dirt and poured water over the top of it, making sure it was out.

Leaving the Circle of Stones that night, I felt different. I'd let go of something cherished, and though it pained me, I suddenly felt older—and stronger. Looking at my brother and Louie, I knew the same was true for them. I saw it in their faces. This quest that we'd started on, it was already changing us.

30

LORETTA

An Important Morning at Home

I was exhausted. The kind of tired that made your body feel heavy. But skipping Dad's breakfast was not an option and would only raise suspicion—not what we wanted or needed. I pulled myself out of bed and fixed my covers. Out of habit, I looked for Blankie to put in my backpack before I remembered and felt a tinge of sadness. On the plus side, I'd still slept like a rock without him.

I ventured down to the kitchen, surprised to see my brother wasn't there yet. But Dad was. He was making a pot of coffee and—no surprise—singing along to a Conway Twitty ballad. He crooned a few lines to me when I walked in.

Hello, darlin'
Nice to see you
It's beeen a long tiiime

I rolled my eyes and plopped into my chair.

Dad laughed and turned down the music. "Not often that you're down here before your brother," he said.

I nodded. "Better keep an eye on him. He's turning into a rebellious teenager."

Dad snorted. "I have an appointment this morning, so you okay if we just do cereal?"

"Sure," I agreed.

"Thanks." He went to the cabinet for our bowls.

"You have an appointment on Saturday?" I asked, after thinking about that.

"Yes. I'm actually interviewing somebody for a possible assistant position," he said, glancing back at me.

"Really?"

"Yes. You and your mother have worn me down."

"'Bout time."

"'Bout time," he mimicked.

"What? You need the help."

He shrugged. "We'll see. Mom's covering a shift for one of the other vets this morning, so I figured I could do the interview."

He placed our bowls and spoons on the table, then grabbed the boxes of cereal from the pantry and the milk from the fridge. Before sitting down, he went to refill his cup of joe. Waylon finally strode in just then, quietly slipping into his chair. When Dad turned around and saw my brother sitting across from me, his jaw practically hit the floor—his coffee did! He slopped it everywhere.

"Son of a nutcracker!" he hollered, shaking his hand where the hot brew had burned him.

Waylon's ponytail! It had never even occurred to me that Mom and Dad would see it missing—obviously! Naturally, there would be questions. Especially from Dad! Asking questions was his job—and then analyzing the answers. So our responses had better be clever—and careful.

Dad cleaned up his mess and joined us. "Must be you weren't kidding when you said rebellious teenager," he whispered to me after taking his seat.

I couldn't help it. I smirked.

Dad placed his mug on the table and looked at my brother. "Well, what did you do?"

"Cut my hair off," Waylon replied.

Good safe answer, I thought.

Dad made a face. "I can see that. What I'm wondering is why."

Waylon shrugged. "It was time."

Ooh, good one, I cheered.

Dad made another face. "And what made you decide that?"

Ugh, tough follow-up question.

Waylon shrugged again.

Yes! Perfect non-answer answer!

"I'm not sure that answer is going to satisfy your mother," Dad replied.

True.

Another shoulder shrug from Waylon. Yikes, he really was playing rebellious teenager this morning.

"I get the feeling you two are up to something," Dad said. "I suggest you consider filling me in so I can help with Mom. If I don't have anything to tell her, then I can't promise I'll be able to keep her out of your hair—even your short hair," he added, and snickered.

Ugh. Leave it to Dad to come up with a great counter-argument.

"You can't let her get involved," Waylon pleaded.

Dad was the one to shrug now. "Then you'd better start talking."

Careful. Minimal information, I urged.

"I sacrificed my hair as an offering to the Forest Spirits," Waylon blurted.

My shoulders sagged. *So much for careful,* I thought. *Apparently, we're trying brutally honest instead.*

Dad blinked.

"Loretta sacrificed Blankie," Waylon blurted next, throwing me under the bus.

And there went any hope for minimal information. Suddenly, my brother was suffering from a case of diarrhea of the mouth. I glared at him.

"Okay," my father said after taking a second to mull that over. "I don't need to mention Blankie to Mom unless she asks."

Thank you. At least he was smarter than my stupid brother.

"But I'm not sure telling her to relax because your hair was an offering to the Forest Spirits is the best approach either. You'd better give me more."

Waylon and I looked at each other. Do we tell him about the box or not? That was the question.

My brother opened his mouth, but before he spilled everything, I cut him off. "Not a word," I ordered, silencing him.

I turned to Dad and gave him the best explanation I could think of, falling back on *The Goonies* for help. Ever see it? You need to. Such a great movie! Anyways, I turned to him and said, "You know how in *The Goonies* they find a treasure map and then go on a big hunt trying to find One-Eyed Willy's lost riches?"

Dad nodded and smiled. He loved that movie.

"Well, we found something similar. Not a treasure map, more like directions to a game." (*Oh, that was good. Calling it a game makes it sound harmless.*) "It's an adventure game, and making a sacrifice was the first task on our quest," I explained.

"And what's next?" he asked.

Again, my brother opened his mouth, but I beat him to it. "We can't tell you." I didn't know if that was going to fly, still, I had to give it a try.

"I'm not sure I like that answer," Dad said.

"All I can say is that we are being safe and everything is legal," I replied.

"Well, that's a relief," he scoffed.

"If the worst thing that happens is Waylon loses his ponytail, then Mom should be happy, not upset," I reasoned.

Dad grinned. "Now that's a great point," he said, sounding proud of my debate skills. "I think that's what I'll tell your mother."

He picked up his mug and sipped his coffee. I breathed a sigh of relief. Maybe we were going to get off the hook—not!

After another sip, he set his mug back down. "So I'm guessing my missing ladder has something to do with your adventures."

I almost spit my Cheerios across the table. Waylon and I glanced at each other.

"Yes, I noticed. A boomer wasn't born last night," he teased.

"We'll return it when we're done," I promised.

"I know you will. I'm not worried about the ladder, but I am still a little worried about my two adventurers, so here's what I need from you. I need you to promise me that if you get into any kind of trouble, that if you need any help whatsoever, you'll come to me right away."

Waylon and I nodded. That sounded fair. "Promise," we said.

Dad's watch beeped. "My interview. I almost forgot."

Thank goodness, I thought. *Maybe the Forest Spirits are helping?*

Dad added a splash of cream to his cup and refilled his coffee. On his way out of the kitchen, he gave us his famous parting words: "Don't do anything I wouldn't do."

What was that even supposed to mean? I shook my head.

"Now what?" I said to Waylon.

"Now I'm going back to bed. I need to rest up before my rite of passage."

"What?!" I shrieked. "You've already got that planned too?"

"No, but I'm starting to think about it. The Forest Spirits will make it clear soon enough, and when they do, I want to be ready."

My brother placed his bowl in the sink and left. I took care of putting away the cereal and loading the dishwasher. I couldn't even begin to imagine what Waylon would conjure up for his rite of passage, but I had no doubt it was going to be every bit as daring as our sacrifices. I just hoped the spirits took their time in revealing it to him. I needed a break after last night. In the meantime, more sleep did sound good—and maybe a movie. *The Goonies* seemed like a good pick.

31

WAYLON

Dinner Talk

As promised, Dad took care of talking to Mom about my hair before she saw it. I wasn't sure what he did and didn't tell her, but he did a good job because she didn't pepper me with questions. And that was a relief because Loretta had made it very clear I was not to tell Mom anything. How're you supposed to answer questions without telling anything? I'd tried that with Dad and did okay at first, but then I cracked.

"Waylon, I just want to say that I'm a big fan of the new haircut," Mom told me at dinner that night.

"Me too," my sister agreed.

"I'll miss the Willie Nelson resemblance," Dad admitted, "but now you're sporting my handsomeness."

"Oh, brother," Loretta groaned.

"So, Mr. Handsome, did you want to thank me for hiring that landscape crew yet?" Mom asked. "They did a great job on the yard again today."

"Mmm," Dad moaned. He still hadn't managed to get his mower up and running.

At the mention of the landscape crew, I glanced at Loretta to gauge her reaction. She remained disinterested. Luckily, my sister had been so engrossed in her movie when the guys showed up earlier that she never bothered looking out her window. I wasn't about to tell her who I'd seen running the weed eater because then she would've gone berserk. She would just need to discover for herself that Leon Hurd was mowing our lawn these days.

"And how about the interview? How did that go?" Mom asked next. Rather than grilling me like I'd feared, she was putting Dad on the spot. I felt sorry for him, but it was better him than me.

"I didn't like her," Dad replied.

"What? Why not?"

He hesitated.

"Why not?" Mom pressed.

Dad sighed. "Because she didn't appreciate my country music. First thing she did was make a remark about how listening to Hank Williams could be considered cruel and unusual punishment."

"Ha!" Loretta laughed.

"So you didn't hire her?" Mom asked.

"No, I didn't hire her!" Dad exclaimed. "I cut the interview short. I can't be expected to work with someone who speaks such blasphemy."

Mom shook her head. "Fine," she huffed. "But you're

going to schedule more interviews because you're getting an assistant."

Dad didn't say anything to that. Mom had put her foot down and that was it.

Landscape crews and interviews aside, I was just relieved to make it through dinner without my hair consuming the entire conversation. Mom, Dad, and Loretta all seemed to like my new look, and I was happy to say thank you and leave it at that. Unfortunately, not everyone else was so kind when they saw me tailless.

32

WAYLON

The Awesomeness of Penelope Grows

P.E. Bubba had plenty to say about my new look when he saw me at camp on Tuesday. I was walking with Penelope on our way to the robotics building when we crossed paths with him.

"'Bout time you cut that hippie hair," he said. "Too bad you don't look any tougher without it. But there's nothing you can do about that since you got stuck with your father's wimp genes."

He guffawed at his own dumb joke and then continued on his way. Loretta would've lost it if she'd heard that, but I wasn't her—and neither was Penelope.

"He'd make a good duck, don't you think? He waddles instead of walks," she said.

I grinned. "A duck with hemorrhoids," I replied.

"Eww," she groaned, and grimaced.

I laughed.

"Sorry he's mean to you," she said after we started walking again.

"It's okay. I don't let it bother me."

"I know how it feels. Kids used to pick on me all the time. I'll admit, I didn't do myself any favors by being a know-it-all and tattletale when I was younger, and add to that the fact that I'm small and have different interests than most, and let the teasing begin."

I remembered her comment at the library about animals not being judgmental like people. "I'm small too," I said. "And what different interests?"

"How many second and third graders do you know who prefer opera and are vegetarian? And I am the only girl at robotics camp, in case you didn't notice."

I stopped on the steps in front of the robotics building. "I noticed, and I think that's cool," I replied. "And I'm not vegetarian, but I think that's cool too. And I'm stuck listening to my father's old-time country music, so opera sounds good to me."

She giggled. "Thanks."

"But you said used to. Kids *used* to pick on you. What changed?"

She leaned on the stair railing. "Used to," she repeated, "until I did a board-breaking demonstration at our school talent show. I'm still not sure if it was my kicks and punches or the way I screamed *Hi-ya* that scared my tormenters most, but they started leaving me alone after that."

My eyes got big. "So you think I should break boards in front of P.E.?"

"Do you know karate or tae kwon do?" she asked, sounding excited about the possibility.

"No."

She giggled again. "That's okay. I've been thinking about how we can teach him a lesson and I think I've got it. Even if his bullying doesn't bother you, it bothers me. We owe him for getting you wet."

My eyes got bigger. "You want to—"

"Set a trap," she said.

"I love traps!" I exclaimed.

"Shhh!" She brought her finger to her lips and looked around. "So do I," she whispered, "especially really sneaky ones."

I swallowed. "What did you have in mind?"

"The car catcher."

Two things happened right then: (1) I got hit with the idea for my rite of passage, and (2) even though I had no clue what the car catcher was, I knew Penelope was the coolest girl I'd ever met. (Please don't tell Loretta I said that. She might get upset. But she's my sister, so she didn't really count anyways.)

Penelope climbed the last few steps and then paused outside the entrance. "Want to meet at the library tomorrow to go over the plan?"

"Sure," I said, pulling the door open for us.

"Great. I'll be there at eleven o'clock. And for what it's worth, I like your new haircut. It was a worthy sacrifice."

I grinned and then followed her inside.

That was it. All of a sudden, I was sneaking out at night without my parents knowing, and now I was sneaking off without Loretta. With that many risks, something was bound to go bad—but that wasn't stopping me.

33

LORETTA

Waylon Disappears—Again!

Forget P.E. Bubba and Leon Hurd; it was Waylon who I had to keep an eye on. I saw him talking to that girl again after camp, which I didn't like one bit, but the real kicker was when he disappeared again on Wednesday.

I went to ask Dad if he knew where Waylon had gone, but my father was in the middle of his second interview, and he had one cardinal rule: Unless there's a fire or someone is dying, NEVER interrupt him when he's with someone in his office. So that left me with no choice but to investigate the matter on my own. The last time my brother had pulled this stunt, he claimed he'd been at the library, so I decided to start there.

I shoved my feet in my sneakers and grabbed my water bottle and bike helmet, and then I set out for Stevens Library. Without Waylon slowing me down, I made it there faster than normal. I rounded the corner and skidded to a stop. My brother's bike was parked in the rack—next to the one with ribbons dangling off the handle grips.

I took my helmet off and wiped my brow. Then I leaned my bike against the wall, away from the one with ribbons, and walked around to the back of the building. If Waylon was here with that girl, then it was likely they'd be in the upstairs section where there were tables and computers and talking was allowed. I chose to enter through the lower level so that I had a better chance of sneaking up on them.

As I neared the top of the stairs, I began scanning the area, but I didn't see them anywhere. That didn't mean they weren't here, only that they were probably on the other side of the room. I hurried from the top step to the nearest stacks and hid among the books. From there, I moved to the end of the row and peeked around the corner.

My heart dropped. There really isn't any other way to describe what I felt. It actually hurt. Waylon was sitting with that girl at the chess table, a big smile on his face. If any other person in the world had betrayed me like that, you can bet I would've marched right over and punched his daylights out—but this was my brother, my twin brother, who'd been by my side since the beginning. I just turned around and left.

I got back on my bike and started for home. The ride to the library might've been easy, but my pedals weren't moving very fast now. They felt heavy. The opposite of how anger can give you a surge of adrenaline and power your muscles, having my heart stomped had completely zapped my strength.

When I made it home, I dumped my bike in the garage

and went straight to my room. I thought about waiting for Waylon and confronting him like I did the last time he'd disappeared on me—but I didn't. If I put my brother in that position, I knew he'd just lie to me more, and I'd had enough for one day.

I stayed in my room until my parents called me for dinner. Mom and Dad did most of the talking after we sat down, which was fine by me. Mom was eager to hear about Dad's interview—until she learned it didn't go well. Again. This time it was because the woman seemed to be an obsessive nose picker. The thought of her touching his files after digging for gold was more than he could handle.

"She just kept going back for more," Dad said. "She couldn't stop. It was disgusting."

Needless to say, it was a short interview. And it was a short dinner for me. I told my parents I wasn't feeling well—which was more or less the truth—and asked to be excused.

Unfortunately, I didn't know how to fix what I was feeling. What was I supposed to do? Beat my brother up? Beat that girl up? Now there was a thought. Sadly, I knew that wouldn't make everything better. In fact, it would probably only make everything worse.

I went to bed early, hoping the Forest Spirits would help me out—but I should've known better. I'd had too many chats with my father. A person can only hold on to hurt for so long before it begins its metamorphosis, growing and changing into anger—deep bottled-up anger that eventually explodes.

34

LORETTA

No Camp

I stayed home from camp on Thursday after telling my parents I still wasn't feeling well. Mom didn't question me. Faking my way out of something wasn't my style, though I did enjoy *Ferris Bueller's Day Off.* Ever see that movie? Classic. I just didn't want to catch my brother with that girl again. Catch them leaning their heads close together and talking and laughing. Not so soon.

The one benefit to being fake sick was that I got to stay in bed with my laptop and watch movies all day long. Contracts didn't apply when you were under the weather. I watched the first three *Jurassic Parks.* I wanted something that I'd already seen and knew the ending to. I missed Blankie, but the movies helped me forget things for a while—until Waylon got home. After grabbing a snack, my brother came into my room to check on me. Nice of him, but that wasn't going to make me forget.

"How're you feeling?" he asked.

I sat up. "Okay."

"You look fine."

"What do you know?!" I shot back. "Maybe I needed a personal day."

His face scrunched. He took a bite of his snack, a celery stalk slathered with hummus and topped with raisins, then offered me a taste.

"Gross!" I replied. "Since when do you eat that stuff?"

He shrugged. "Thought I'd try a healthy option."

"Weird."

"It's not weird," he snapped, getting agitated.

Now that was weird. Waylon never got mad. Why was he being so touchy about celery?

"Sor-ry," I said.

He shoved the rest of it in his mouth. Like that was going to prove anything. I grabbed *Entertainment Weekly* from my nightstand and thumbed through it while he chomped away.

"I've decided on my rite of passage," he informed me after swallowing.

I tossed the magazine aside and sat up straighter. "Already?" With everything else that had happened over the last few days, I'd forgotten all about rites of passage. "What is it?" I asked (even though I wasn't sure I wanted to know).

"I can't tell you, but you'll learn soon enough. I want to start tomorrow night."

"Tomorrow?"

"The idea came to me at camp."

"Oh, yeah. Was it the Forest Spirits or that girl who revealed it to you?"

Waylon's eyes narrowed. I could see him trying to figure out how much I knew about "that girl."

"Her name is Penelope," he said.

"I don't care. Did she put you up to this?"

"What? No!" he shouted. "Penelope isn't even in our club."

That was true, but I still didn't trust her—or my brother. "Well, I don't have my rite of passage ready yet, so you're just gonna have to wait."

"Doesn't matter," Waylon said. "We can't attempt our tests on the same night, anyway. That's not how this part works. A rite of passage is a significant challenge, one that represents your entry into manhood or womanhood, if you conquer it," he explained. "I'll go tomorrow night and you and Louie will go later."

A significant challenge? Manhood and womanhood? What was he thinking this time?

"Tomorrow night," Waylon repeated.

I nodded, and then he left. After he was gone, I squeezed my pillow because I didn't have Blankie. The hurt wasn't going away.

35

LORETTA

Waylon's Rite of Passage

I was steaming mad with Waylon, but that didn't mean I was ready to see him die. Leon Hurd was still out there. The plan to toughen my brother up was still the plan. That hadn't changed. His rite of passage was going to be his next Mr. Miyagi training exercise—at least that was what I told myself to help round up the courage to go.

Come Friday at midnight, the two of us executed another flawless escape. And even though our arrival at Louie's house wasn't planned, we spotted him peering out his window, waiting for us. Waylon looked at me and grinned.

"The Forest Spirits," he whispered.

"Whatever," I groaned. "Let's go."

We gripped Dad's ladder and dashed across the backyard. After getting Louie down, we immediately set out for the fortress. No time for small talk. This was all business. (Don't be misled; that didn't mean it was easy.) Even though we'd done this before, traveling through the forest at night was still super freaky. I'd seen too many movies, and this was the part where something bad happens—and something bad did happen. We weren't attacked by the bobcat if that's what you were thinking, but I tripped and fell and smacked my knee against a rock. We didn't have that far left to go, so I told Louie and my brother that I was okay, but it hurt like heck.

"We're here tonight because the Forest Spirits have revealed my rite of passage," Waylon announced after we'd gathered inside our hideout and the medicine man had cleaned and tended to my knee. A small bandage and I was all set.

"What exactly does that mean?" Louie asked, packing up his medical kit.

"A rite of passage is a significant challenge, one that represents your entry into manhood or womanhood, if you conquer it," Waylon explained, repeating the same thing he'd told me. "Different cultures have different rituals," he continued, "but one thing is for certain: it needs to be daring. Young Native American boys could be challenged to go out and kill a buffalo with nothing but their knife!" he exclaimed, getting excited. "The Maasai tribe of Africa challenged their boys to go out into the savanna to hunt and kill a lion!"

Louie lost it after hearing that. "You're out of your mind!" he shouted. "Let me guess, you want me to hunt and kill a bear with just my hands. Well, you can forget it. You can count me out this time."

"Louie, calm down," I ordered. "You don't have to kill a bear." I was putting the kibosh on that idea before

Waylon actually started to entertain the possibility. "Not all challenges are as extreme as the Maasai," I told him. (I didn't have any good examples right then, but that had to be true.) "And besides, tonight is about Waylon's rite of passage, not yours."

He nodded and took a puff from his inhaler, but worry still etched his face.

I turned to my brother. "Let's hear what you've got planned."

Waylon leaned forward and rubbed his hands together. "I'm not going to kill any animal," he said. "Killing a creature for no reason would be disrespectful. You should only kill one if you're going to use all of its various parts for survival. So instead, I plan to catch and release one."

"This isn't fishing," I groaned. "That won't count."

"I'm not talking about fishing," Waylon shot back. "I'm talking about a bobcat."

"A bobcat!" Louie cried. "Ohh."

"Yes, a bobcat," Waylon repeated. "We know there's one around here, and I'm going to catch it. It's not a lion, but I think it qualifies as dangerous enough, especially since I'm going to release it after I trap it."

"Waylon, don't you think this might be a bit far-fetched?" I said. "You don't want to set yourself up for failure. I mean, seriously, a bobcat?"

"You agree, then?" he countered. "Catching and releasing a bobcat would be a formidable challenge, one worthy of qualifying as my rite of passage?"

"Yes, but—"

"No buts. I'm going to do it."

I went to object again but then stopped. What did I care if my brother succeeded or not? And I definitely didn't expect him to succeed. The important thing here was the fact that what he was proposing had the makings of a huge Mr. Miyagi undertaking, just as I'd hoped. "Suit yourself," I said. "Go for it."

"Ohh," Louie moaned again.

Waylon beamed. "Okay," he said. "One requirement in any rite of passage is that it be completed alone, in solitude. I'll need the rest of tonight and all day tomorrow to build and set my trap. Loretta, I'll need you to take care of Mom and Dad. You and Louie can meet me back here at midnight."

"Fine," I replied.

"Waylon," Louie croaked, "suppose you do catch a bobcat. How're you going to release it without getting killed?"

"Don't worry. I've got it all figured out." He pulled up his pant leg, revealing his newest tattoo, that of a rabbit which he'd positioned on his calf. "The rabbit outsmarts the bobcat," he said, making it sound that simple.

Judging by Louie's face, it wasn't that simple for him. Me? I still didn't think he stood a chance at capturing the animal, so why fret about its release?

"It's settled, then," I said. "We'll see you tomorrow night. This meeting's adjourned."

I crawled out of the fortress and stood. Louie and Waylon followed.

"Good luck, Waylon," Louie whispered.

My brother nodded and saluted, and then Louie and I marched off. I accompanied Louie back to his house because there was no way I was walking through the woods on my own. After dropping him off, I took the roads home.

Louie returned to his bedroom full of worry that night. I crawled under the covers feeling concerned, but not for my brother. Waylon was smart and would be fine. I was more concerned about Mom and Dad and what I was going to tell them. And a tiny part of me was also getting concerned about my own rite of passage—because my brother had just set the bar pretty high.

36

WAYLON

Building My Trap

I huddled inside the fortress after my sister and Louie left. It would be near impossible to accomplish much in the dead of night, even with my headlamp, so I settled on reviewing my plan. I had to keep my mind busy; otherwise my imagination was likely to take over. A dark forest was spooky, but being alone in a dark forest was next-level scary. I had to put my faith in the Forest Spirits to protect me and keep me safe, and overcome my fear. That was all part of my rite of passage. Easier said than done.

I continued to jump and flinch at every noise. I had to pee as bad as a racehorse, but my will to hold it and stay safe inside the fortress was stronger than my urge to go. (I didn't have that much faith in the Forest Spirits.) Fortunately, I managed to doze off after a while. I awoke at the first signs of dawn, when light was just beginning to break through the trees. It was time to get to work.

The first thing I needed to do was determine the optimal site for my trap. That might sound trivial, but it was one of the most important parts. You could have the best trap ever built, but if you put it in the wrong location, it would never work.

I adjusted my headlamp and began inspecting my surroundings, searching for any signs of animal activity: tracks, rubbings, claw markings, paths, dens, scat. You get the idea. I hoped to find a place not too far from the fortress, but I also needed to make sure there was a strong tree nearby. (I would need that before I got done.)

After several trips around the area, I settled on a spot past the Circle of Stones, roughly twenty feet beyond the edge of the clearing. There were two well-traveled trails leading to and from the location.

Once I'd selected the site, it was time to get building. The design I had in mind would likely be considered a drop trap, but it also had cage and snare attributes incorporated. The cage was where I needed to start.

With my hatchet, I began the hard work of making stakes, similar to what I did when building our fortress, only this time the stakes needed to be the same length and cut with one end coming to a very sharp point for stabbing into the ground—that was important. Using my survival line, I tethered the stakes to the top and bottom cross-posts. Then I added a roof and did more knotting and securing. It took me all morning, but I managed to build a solid cage that was designed to fall over the top of my bobcat, thus trapping it. I'd also succeeded in polishing off my water and the lone PB&J that I'd packed, but there wasn't much I could do about that.

After drinking my last swallow, I decided to attach a heavy flat rock to the top of my cage, as an added measure. Without the additional weight, I worried a ticked-off bobcat might have the strength to flip the cage over and escape. I was hopeful the rock would prevent that—unless I caught a bobcat as big as a bear. Or an actual bear. How cool would that be! Anything was possible with the Forest Spirits in my corner.

I moved on to camouflaging next. Again, similar to what we did with the fortress, I weaved leafy branches in and out of the stakes. And lastly, I tied a long piece of my thickest survival line to the middle of the roof. At this point, my cage was ready to be suspended in the air, but not before I constructed the ground components of my trap.

The ground components were critical. To function properly, this element required precision. First, I cut identical notches into the sides of my last two remaining stakes, and then I drove the stakes into the ground, six inches apart from each other, notches facing inward. Next, I took a smaller but strong stick, cut exact to fit in between the two stakes, and tied the thick survival line that I'd attached to my cage around the middle of it. This short stick was called the trigger stick, and it was the key to my entire operation.

I had a batch of fresh blisters to show for my efforts, but so far, so good. It was finally time to set my trap. I took the trigger stick and tossed it up and over a solid branch that hung above me. (This was why I needed that strong tree nearby.) The idea was simple. Using the mechanism of a basic pulley, I was going to pull down on the trigger stick line, thus lifting the cage into the air. When I had the cage to a desired height, I was going to roll up the extra line like you do when flying a kite and slide the trigger stick into position between my two notched stakes. The cage would stay suspended until something knocked the trigger stick free. But what would do that? And why?

This was where being clever came into play. All I had to do was slather the trigger stick with the world's best-known bait—peanut butter. I'd brought two travel packets with me to do the job. There wasn't an animal alive that didn't love the taste of peanut butter. Mr. Bobcat wouldn't be able to resist. He'd begin licking the bait, carefully at first, and then more and more aggressively after being overcome with its delicious flavor. It wouldn't take long before he knocked the trigger stick free, causing the cage to drop over the top of him, and wa-la. Trapped!

My design was textbook and my plan bulletproof—in theory. Unfortunately, putting theory into action isn't always so easy or straightforward. The pulley concept was a good one, but I wasn't near strong enough to make it work. After all the hatchet swinging and building that I'd done, I couldn't hoist the cage off the ground. Tie more line to it and maximize the number of pulleys? Not a bad idea, except I was out of line. Sneaking home to get more would be considered cheating, and besides that, there wasn't any at home.

I slumped against the tree. There wasn't anything I could do. I'd have to wait until Loretta and Louie joined me, which meant my trap wouldn't be ready. That was it. I'd already failed my rite of passage.

"I'm sorry I let you down, Forest Spirits," I whispered. "I tried."

I hung my head in shame and closed my eyes. I was exhausted, but more than anything I felt dejected.

A minute, maybe two, passed in silence, and then I heard the unmistakable sound of something approaching. I sat up and listened. There it was again.

I scrambled to my backpack and quickly loaded my slingshot. Were the spirits delivering the beast to me early?

"I wasn't going to kill you, Mr. Bobcat, but if you step into view, I'll have no choice but to shoot your eye out," I whispered in warning.

I steadied my breathing and pulled back my stone. I waited. And then the last thing I ever expected to see stepped into view.

"Dad? What're you doing here?" I said, lowering my weapon.

"Hi there," he said. "I thought you might need a little nourishment. You've been out here for quite a while." He handed me a paper bag with a sandwich, granola bar, apple, and water bottle inside.

"Thanks. I am hungry," I admitted.

"You should be. It's almost four o'clock."

"Did Loretta put you up to this?" I asked after guzzling the water and biting into the sandwich.

"No. Nope. She didn't say much actually, only that you left the house real early, that you were determined to spend a full day and night out here because you wanted to be like Sam Gribley in *My Side of the Mountain*. I had a sneaky suspicion you were tackling your next task but didn't ask. It took a fair amount of coaxing to get Mom to accept the overnight part as it was. She's the one who insisted I check on you."

Good thing neither of you knows I've already been out here for one night, I thought, and grinned. "Thanks."

"Wow! That's quite the cage," he remarked, eyeing my creation. "You built that from scratch?"

"Yeah. Just me and my trusty hatchet."

"Impressive. You've really become a skilled builder."

I shrugged. "Too bad it won't do me any good."

"Why? What's wrong with it?"

I shoved the last of granola bar into my mouth and explained my design to Dad and what I was trying to accomplish.

"Well, I'm here now. I can help you get it set," he said.

"Really?"

"Yeah. C'mon."

I lifted my chin and looked to the sky. The Forest Spirits hadn't delivered the bobcat, but they'd brought me help. Dad grabbed the line with me, and together we pulled. Even with two of us it was a struggle. My cage was legit. But we got it hoisted and my trigger stick into position.

"Phew," Dad said, wiping his brow. "What do you hope to catch anyway?"

"Bobcat," I answered.

"Oh." He gave me a look but didn't say anything more.

It was fine if he was skeptical. I was confident. The spirits wouldn't have bothered sending me help if my trap wasn't going to work.

"Well, I guess I can head back home now," Dad said. "Good luck. And don't worry, I won't mention that I gave you a hand to anyone. That's between you and the Forest Spirits."

I smiled. "Thanks, Dad. And thanks for the food."

"Be safe. And don't do anything I wouldn't do," he said.

I shook my head, still smiling. "See you later."

I watched as he walked off, vanishing behind the trees. Then I looked at my trap and took a deep breath, filling my lungs and letting it out slowly. I was ready. I had a few hours to rest, but come darkness, I was going to catch that bobcat.

37

LORETTA

Trapped!

Louie and I joined Waylon at midnight, exactly as planned. Wasting no time, my brother led us to his trap. He was excited to show it off; plus, he needed to check on it. In a low whisper, Waylon explained the concepts behind his creation and how it was supposed to work. I speak for Louie and myself when I say we were amazed. It was the stuff of a true mastermind, but we were also relieved to find the trap empty. Waylon, on the other hand, was disappointed—but only slightly; the night was still young.

It was unlikely anything would venture into the area with us around, so we made our way back to the fortress. Waylon planned to continue checking on his trap every hour, on the hour. Needless to say, it was going to be a long night, so it was a good thing I came prepared. I pulled out a box of crackers and a deck of cards. The three of us huddled inside the safety of our hideout, playing Uno and enjoying the snacks, until it was time to investigate again.

The trap remained empty at one o'clock. It was still untouched at two o'clock. And three o'clock. But come four o'clock, when the three of us wore heavy eyes and weren't as sure-footed, it was a different story.

"My cage is on the ground!" Waylon exclaimed, trying to maintain a whisper. "Something's taken the bait."

"Is it the bobcat?" Louie asked, his voice shaking.

"I don't know, but I'm going to see."

I inched forward, wondering if I should follow.

"No," Waylon said, putting up his hand. "This is my rite of passage. I have to go alone."

There was no use arguing, not that I wanted to. This was how my brother needed it to be, but that didn't mean I wasn't scared for him—even if I was still angry with him for betraying me.

Looking back on it now, let's just say I'm glad Waylon made us stay. His rabbit may have outsmarted the bobcat, but he was no match for the critter under that cage.

38

WAYLON

Shot!

I adjusted my headlamp and crept forward, leaving Loretta and Louie safely hidden in the bushes. As I neared my trap, an intense hissing ensued. I smiled. There was no doubt: I'd caught something. But what? Would a bobcat hiss? I couldn't see past the extensive camouflaging that I'd given the cage, so I didn't know.

I continued inching my way along. As I drew closer, my smile faded. I knew a lot about animals, but the noises coming from under my cage were unlike anything I'd ever heard. The hissing morphed into a mix of deep guttural sounds and spitting. Whatever lurked on the other side was madder than the devil and almost certain to attack me when I tried to release it.

I was wide awake now. My mouth had gone dry, but my palms were wet with sweat. I reached for my trusty slingshot and loaded it. The feel of it in my hands helped to steady my breathing, but I prayed I didn't need to use it.

I scanned the area, searching for the trigger stick. The safest and smartest way to free the animal would be to reel in the trigger stick line until it lifted an edge of the cage off the ground. Unfortunately, that could be chalked up as another good idea in theory that wasn't going to work. It wasn't even an option. Whatever was inside the cage hadn't knocked the trigger stick loose from the notch to spring the trap; instead, it had chewed through the survival line. And just my luck, the line had fallen inside the cage when it came down off the tree limb, so now I had to find a different way to lift the cage and free the animal—without getting myself killed!

I continued scanning the area, looking for anything that might help. My best option was a long, forked limb that I'd discarded when doing the camouflage. I pocketed my slingshot and dragged the limb over to the cage. The trapped animal's hissing grew wild, and then it began ramming against the sides of the cage. It was crazy mad.

My hands shook and my teeth chattered, but I put faith in the Forest Spirits and pressed onward with my new plan. I grasped the limb and wedged its forked end against one of the cage's top cross-posts. I spread my feet and took a strong stance. This was it.

I took a breath and leaned into the branch with all of my weight. I barely got the bottom edge lifted off the ground, and the captive streaked out. The angry critter was so disoriented that it didn't know which way to go. It ran one way, then the other. I screamed and fumbled to load my slingshot, but I didn't stand a chance. The black-and-white ball of fur spit and spun around, lifting its tail and taking aim with its rear end. I didn't need my headlamp to see that I was a goner.

Skunks can spray with deadly accuracy up to fifteen feet away—maybe more! This nasty bugger did not disappoint. His blast shot me square in my chest and face. Luckily, I knew enough to close my eyes—the eyes are where a skunk aims, hoping to blind its predator—but not my mouth. I was still too busy screaming. The spray coated my tongue. I dropped to my knees, coughing and gagging as that nasty varmint finally made its getaway.

"Waylon, are you okay?" Loretta called. She and Louie came running.

I couldn't answer. It was horrible. The taste was a hundred times worse than the smell. Loretta tried, but patting me on the back didn't do anything. I kept coughing and gagging and then I lost control and vomited—not once, but twice. From there, it just got worse. I couldn't catch my breath.

"Waylon!" Loretta shrieked. She was scared now.

Louie knelt next to me and my puke and stuck his inhaler into my mouth and gave me a puff. Then another. And one more for good measure.

"Slow and easy breaths," he coached me. "In and out, nice and easy." His voice sounded funny, but I listened to him. He inhaled and exhaled alongside me, and eventually I was able to regain control. He handed me his water next, and I rinsed my mouth and spit. I spit and spit and spit, until I could spit no more. Then I wiped my eyes and slowly got to my feet.

"Thanks," I said.

"You made me the healer," he reminded me, showing off his medicine man tattoo. I saw why his voice sounded funny now. He had his nose plugged.

"You reek," Loretta groaned, plugging hers too. Apparently, she was done feeling sorry for me.

I didn't have the energy to argue. I turned and stumbled my way back to the fortress with Loretta and Louie granting me plenty of space.

"Sorry, Waylon," Louie said. "I don't want to get too close because I can't risk smelling like you when I get home."

I nodded. I understood. I was gonna have a problem smelling like me when I got home, but there wasn't anything I could do about that.

We gathered our gear and set out for Louie's house, hustling because it was nearing dawn now. My adventure had been a terrifying thrill ride with the highs and lows of an exhilarating roller coaster. My mistake was in thinking the ride was over—it wasn't. The best was yet to come.

39

LORETTA

Fireworks

We reached Louie's house before the sun was up, but not by much. It had already been a night like no other. The suspense and danger of a killer action movie—but we weren't done yet. Such a night called for a grand finale— and there were some real fireworks on the way.

I steadied Dad's ladder with my free hand while Waylon used both of his. He was lucky that his nose had gone numb and he wasn't stuck smelling his own putrid stink.

"Louie, you left your window open," I groaned after glancing up. "You've had a cold draft blowing into your room all night. We're lucky your parents didn't wake up already."

"I thought I closed it," he apologized.

"Never mind. Just get going."

Louie started his climb but then stopped when he was only a few rungs off the ground. "Um, congratulations on your rite of passage, Waylon," he whispered from above.

The fact that my suffering brother even cracked a grin tells you how special Louie was.

"Get going," I told him.

Louie turned and resumed climbing. He was almost to the top when his wild-hair mother suddenly stuck her head out of the opening and glared down at Waylon and me.

"Get away from my son, you devil bandits!" she shrieked. She pulled Louie through the window and slammed it shut.

Waylon and I grabbed Dad's ladder and booked it to the woods. Only after we'd reached cover did we pause to look back. Waylon wasn't taking any chances. He loaded his slingshot and shattered the rest of the lights hanging in the trees nearest us. Darkness was our ally now.

We waited. There was no sign of the woman, but soon we heard her hysterical cries coming from Louie's bedroom.

"I'd rather go on a lion hunt than tangle with her," Waylon whispered.

I nodded. "May the Force be with you, Louie."

"And the Forest Spirits too," Waylon added.

We turned and headed for home.

40

LORETTA

What's That Smell?

I was the first to stumble into the kitchen a mere two hours after making it home from a night of absolute craziness capped off by a predawn mega scare. Mom was already sitting at the table, listening to Dad croon a George Strait song while pouring her a cup of coffee. She looked at me and rolled her eyes.

I smirked and pulled out my chair.

"Good morning," she said, wrinkling her nose.

Uh-oh. Did I stink? I didn't think so, but was there such a thing as white smell like there was white noise? Had my nose grown accustomed to my own stench?

"Good morning," I replied.

Mom didn't say anything more, but I caught Dad peeking in my direction. He grimaced. That was it. We were done for. If I stunk, Waylon . . .

Speak of the devil, here he came. Mom's nose wrinkled extra before my brother even stepped foot in the kitchen. And when he did arrive on the scene, she didn't hold back.

"Ugh," she groaned, plugging her nose in disgust. "Waylon, it's you! What happened?"

He sighed and tried walking to his spot at the table, but Mom stopped him in his tracks. "No!" she objected, putting her hand up. "Honey, I'm sorry, but you smell terrible. You need to take a shower before you come in here."

Waylon turned around, sulking.

"Your trap worked, didn't it?" Dad said, unable to contain his excitement.

Waylon stopped. When he saw Dad smiling, he brightened. "Yeah, but I caught a skunk instead of the bobcat."

"Skunk? Bobcat?!" Mom cried. "What's going on here?" She looked back and forth between Dad and Waylon, waiting for an explanation. They were doomed.

"Lisa, hon, you should've seen the trap your son built," Dad said. "It was incredible. Everything about it was so thought out and smart. From location to concept to design. Everything—except for one small miscalculation."

"What?" Waylon and Mom asked in chorus, though I wasn't sure they were asking for the same reason.

"Bobcats are not hunters that rely on smell," Dad said, "but on keen eyesight. Your peanut butter bait was sure to attract something with a good nose but not good eyes."

"Oh," Waylon mumbled, his voice low, his spirits lower. He was so disappointed in himself.

"But your trap worked!" Dad exclaimed, doing his best to cheer my brother up. "That's awesome!"

Waylon grinned.

"I can't believe you knew about this," Mom growled, shooting daggers at Dad. "You told me he was sleeping in his fort. That was it."

What was it with men thinking they could get away with keeping stuff from us, smarter women? Were they really that dumb?

"Umm . . . I . . . well, maybe . . . sort of," Dad stammered. He was in so much trouble. "But doesn't it sound great?"

"David! He was trying to catch a bobcat! I don't call that great!"

Mom turned on my brother next. "I could've told you everything you needed to know about bobcats, including the fact that the one in our area was captured and relocated. It seems your father neglected to tell you that."

Dad and Waylon were shrinking before my eyes—and Mom was just getting started.

"I want to know why you were building a trap, and why you had to sneak out to join him," she demanded, glaring at me now too. "And why you didn't tell me?" she added, shooting daggers at Dad again.

Dad opened his mouth to offer some feeble explanation but then reverted to something even dumber. He actually chose to sing along with the Waylon Jennings tune that began playing on the radio instead.

Just the good ol' boys
Never meaning no harm

That was as far as he got with that terrible idea before Mom lost it. "You're insufferable!" she roared.

She got up and shoved her chair in. "Waylon, go and get in the shower. I'll drive into the office and get the product we have for treating skunk spray. Just what I wanted to do on my Sunday," she complained on her way out of the kitchen.

It was only Dad and me after that. "Boy, you're in the doghouse now," I said. "Not sure singing to her was your best idea."

"Yeah, maybe not," he agreed. "I'll talk to her when she gets back. Give her some time to cool off."

I thought of Louie's mom when he said that and wondered if time would help her cool off. Somehow, I didn't think so, but I didn't mention any of that to Dad—not then.

"So what's your rite of passage?" he asked.

"I don't know," I admitted, surprised he was even asking after what had just happened.

"Well, it's probably better if you don't tell me. That way I'm not in the position of keeping something from your mother."

I nodded.

"Just do me a favor," he said. "No bobcats and don't do—"

"Anything that you wouldn't do," I finished. "I know."

"Exactly," he said, and smiled.

I got up from the table then. "I think I'll shower and go back to sleep."

"Good idea because you don't smell like roses either. I'll take care of cleaning up."

I stuck my tongue out at him. "Good luck with Mom."

"Don't worry. She can't stay mad at me forever." He began singing again to make his point.

> She's a good-hearted woman in love with a good-timin' man
> She loves him in spite of his ways that she don't understand

Another terrible country song. I shook my head and left. When was he ever going to learn? At least I wouldn't need to worry about any PDA from the boomers for a while. Dad was going to be on the couch.

41

LORETTA

The Car Catcher

Waylon and I had to lie low after his skunk debacle. Mom was still angry with all of us, to the point where I was beginning to worry that both my Mr. Miyagi plans and our late-night adventures could be in jeopardy. Obviously, that was problematic for Waylon's muscles, but it was Louie that had me most concerned. Our friend's fragile predicament was 100 percent our fault. I couldn't stop thinking about him—but that didn't seem to be an issue for my brother.

Needless to say, given our current situation and the fact that I was still not over Waylon lying to me, I was not at all in the mood for his cheery excitement when he came into my room before going to bed on Monday night.

"I can't wait for camp tomorrow. Penelope and I have something awesome planned!" he exclaimed.

My wolf hair raised at the mere mention of the girl's name. "What?" I snarled.

"I can't give you the details, but you're going to love it."

"What is it?" I pressed.

"It was Penelope's idea."

"What?" I growled. I was becoming increasingly agitated with his giddiness about Penelope and her big plans—and his complete disregard for Louie. I was on the verge of exploding and telling my brother exactly how I felt, but he managed to find just the right words to prevent that in his next breath.

Waylon sighed. "It's called the car catcher. It's a trap specially designed for P.E., but that's all I can tell you."

I never thought I'd be so eager to hear about a trap again, but one designed for P.E. was a different story. I didn't push Waylon for any more information, but there was no way I was missing out. For one, I didn't like my brother spending all his time with this Penelope girl; for two, I was the one who had a score to settle with P.E., so if there was a plot to get him, then I was going to be in on it. I went to sleep devising my own plan.

The next morning at camp, I slipped away from the soccer fields by telling my counselor I needed to use the bathroom—an easy con. Instead, I snuck around to the far side of the youth center, where I was safely out of sight from everyone, and then I ran across the road and hid behind the dumpster adjacent to the robotics building. Now all I had to do was wait for Waylon and Penelope to make their move. I didn't have to wait long.

The girl came out first, but not through the front entrance. I didn't even realize she had emerged until she was suddenly crouching next to me behind the dumpster. We stared at each other, both of us alarmed to see the other there, both of us refusing to look away, and neither of us speaking a word. She was lucky Waylon joined us a minute later.

"Loretta, what're you doing here?!" he asked, clearly surprised.

I continued glaring at the girl and said nothing.

"Penelope, this is my sister, Loretta," Waylon explained, introducing me to her.

"Nice to meet you," the girl said, breaking our silence.

"Wish I could say the same. This trap of yours better work," I warned her.

Penelope held my stare. "The car catcher's going to work," she assured me with full confidence—and I believed her.

She unzipped her bag and pulled out a coil of thin silver wire. "This is the only thing we need," she said.

I glanced at my brother. Was she serious?

"I've been studying P.E.'s tendencies," she continued. "Every day he comes and goes from the same special parking spot in his beloved car."

I shrugged. "Yeah, so."

"So today is garbage day," Penelope said, pointing down the road. "And a few of those houses still use the old metal garbage cans."

"Okay. So?"

"So we're going to take this wire and tie it to one of those cans and then run it across the road and tie it to a second one. It's got to be the metal cans," she stressed, "because that'll work best. This wire is thin enough that P.E. won't ever see it, especially because he'll never be expecting it, and it's stiff enough and strong enough that it will stay suspended in the air until a fancy red sports car drives through it like a runner breaking the tape at the finish line."

"And then those garbage cans will come flying in from the sides and smash against his car like a giant pair of cymbals!" Waylon exclaimed.

"Shhh!" Penelope and I scolded.

"Sorry," Waylon murmured, "but this is going to be awesome. It's brilliant."

"Thanks," Penelope said, "but keep your voice down."

"I've got a question," I said, interrupting their little romance. "If we set the trap now, how do we know a different car won't drive through it first? I know it's a one-way road, so we don't have to worry about anyone coming from the other direction, but how can we guarantee P.E. will be the first to hit the trap?"

"I like you, Loretta," Penelope said. "You're all business."

"You can say that again," Waylon remarked.

I punched him in the shoulder.

"P.E. listed his phone number on the camp information sheets," Penelope explained. "As soon as we have the trap set, we call him—from a school phone so that he can't trace the number; I've already found one we can use in the robotics building—and pretend to be from Central

Office. Something has come up and we need him to get there straightaway."

I was impressed. "You've done your homework."

Penelope nodded. "You can't send a man to do a woman's job," she said.

I smiled. It was involuntary, and I couldn't help it. What can I say, I liked this girl—and so did my brother. Waylon gazed at her with equal parts admiration and puppy love. He'd found a girl who was more like him than his own twin sister. That hurt, but now was not the time to dwell on feelings.

"Let's do this," I said, "before somebody notices we've disappeared."

Penelope glanced around, checking to make sure the coast was clear, and then she took off, running down the road. Waylon and I were right behind her.

When we reached the first trash can, she immediately began attaching the wire to the handle, wrapping it around and around. Waylon played lookout while I took the other end of the wire and ran it across the road. I rigged up the second can like I'd seen Penelope doing, making sure to pull the wire taut. The whole operation was over in a matter of minutes. It was so simple, yet so smart—and as we'd soon discover, so effective.

With the wire in position, we raced back to the dumpster. Penelope and Waylon returned to robotics and I scooted off to the soccer fields. If all else went according to plan, it wouldn't be long before P.E. was hurrying to his car.

It went better than planned.

I don't know what Penelope said to P.E. over the phone, or if any call from Central Office would've garnered the same response, but he came running out of his office like he was on fire, and after almost tripping and falling, he got into his car and peeled out of the parking lot. Squealing his tires got everyone's attention, which meant every pair of eyeballs was watching as he sped down the road and tangled with the car catcher. He never saw the wire. He never slowed down.

Those metal cans came flying in from the sides with incredible momentum. It was a direct hit. They crashed into P.E.'s precious car just as Waylon had predicted, like a giant pair of cymbals, and let me tell you, the musical note that rang out sounded glorious.

P.E.'s car came to a screeching halt. Garbage filled the convertible and scattered all over the road. He tumbled out and after taking one look at his Corvette, proceeded to have a meltdown. "No!" he cried. "No!"

Shouts and laughter filled the air all around me.

"Whoa!"

"Wow!"

"Did you see that?!"

Yup, I'd seen it. I thought Waylon's bobcat trap was the best ever, but Penelope's car catcher just took that prize. It was spectacular.

I gazed over the field, taking immense satisfaction in the multitude of campers laughing at P.E. And then who did I see? You guessed it. Leon Hurd stood near the landscaping truck and trailer parked against the curb with his eyes locked on me. He smirked when I saw him. I was the wolf, but I immediately looked away. I couldn't risk giving myself up. The question was, what did he know? There wasn't anything I could do about it now, so I turned and jogged across the field, blending in with all the innocent campers running around, hooting and cheering.

Was it fun? Yes. But it wasn't like we got off scot-free. There were consequences. (More on that later.)

42

LORETTA

Isn't Penelope the Best?

We didn't have a chance to celebrate or even talk about it at camp, not with everyone around, so as soon as we got home Waylon burst into my room, spewing praise for his girlfriend.

"That was incredible!" he exclaimed. "Isn't Penelope the best?"

I'd held it in as long as I could. No more. The wolf lashed out. "You know what, I'm sick of hearing about your little girlfriend," I snapped. And I meant it. What good was being the wolf if I didn't have a pack? Waylon was ready to ditch me for this girl.

I could see he was surprised by my attack, but he didn't hold back either. "Just because you can't make any friends doesn't mean that I'm not supposed to."

"You call yourself a friend?" I shot back. "You're so preoccupied with that girl that you've completely forgotten about Louie. Some friend you are."

"I can't wait for middle school. I'll finally have a chance to get away from you."

That cut deep, but I wasn't about to show it. "Until you need me to save you again," I snarled. "Because if it's not Leon Hurd, it'll be somebody else, and you know it. But don't come crying to me for help. You can ask your girlfriend."

"I will."

"Good."

"You think you're so tough," Waylon said. "You can prove it. Tonight is your rite of passage."

I wasn't expecting that. It came out of nowhere. "Tonight? I don't even have my rite of passage planned," I said.

"I do," Waylon replied.

"I thought it was up to me to choose it."

"Not this time," Waylon said. "Your test has been revealed to me."

"And you think I'm doing it tonight?"

He nodded. "You have to."

"Fine," I huffed. "Bring it on."

"Oh, I will," he promised. Then he turned and stormed out of my room, leaving me standing there.

Between my brother and Penelope, Louie and his mom, and Leon Hurd popping up everywhere I least wanted him to, I was a mess. I was sad on top of angry, on top of confused and scared. Scared of losing my brother to a girl that I actually liked. How was that even possible? Scared for Louie, trapped with his crazy mother. And scared of what Waylon had planned for my rite of passage—because there was no way I could back out of it. No matter what.

43

LORETTA

Mom Stops Us

I dressed in my freshly laundered sneak-out clothes while Waylon was stuck trying to find something new. His skunk attire was history. Mom made him throw it out.

We met outside our bedrooms just before midnight and had nothing to say to one another. I wasn't excited about my impending rite of passage, but I was anxious to check on Louie. It had been too long since we saw him last—even if it had only been a few days. After what happened, I think you can understand how I was feeling. The question was, had it been long enough for his mother to cool off? We were about to find out.

"Going somewhere?" Mom asked from the darkness.

Waylon and I both jumped but held in our screams. We didn't answer, because what were we supposed to say?

"Come in here, please," Mom said.

We stepped into the living room and saw her sitting on the sofa, Dad next to her, only their faces lit by the sliver of moonlight shining through the window. If they weren't our parents, I would've said they were ghosts. It was eerie—the stuff of movies!

"Did you really think I was just going to let you sneak off again after what happened?" Mom's head said.

We still had no answer for her, and Dad was not rushing to our sides this time. Clearly, he was still in the doghouse.

"Well, I'm not," she answered for us.

"Mom, please don't stop us," Waylon begged. He couldn't bear the thought of our quest ending. I could hear it in his voice. "We won't do anything more with animals, I promise."

I glanced at him out the corner of my eye. *What did he have planned?* I worried. Maybe I did want her to stop us.

"I'll admit, I was a bit alarmed when your ponytail and Blankie disappeared, but I can't say I wasn't glad to see that happen," Mom confessed. "So against my better judgment, I let things go. And look at how that turned out. I'm not about to make that mistake again."

Waylon wasn't giving up that easily. "Has Dad told you about our quest?" he asked.

"Yes," Mom replied.

I was actually happy to hear that. If there was more that Dad had kept from her, then his next stop might've been on the curb.

"The directions we found call for us to do certain things at night," Waylon explained, which wasn't entirely true, but that was okay.

"Mom, can I talk to you in private?" I said. I didn't see us getting out of this jam, so I had to take a shot. But let's be clear, I wasn't doing this for Waylon. I did it for Louie.

She rose from the sofa, and we stepped into the kitchen. I told her how I was trying to toughen Waylon up to get him ready for middle school. I told her about the many things we'd already done and how going along with Waylon's nighttime fire ceremonies was part of it. But I never mentioned Louie.

"Your father took me out to your site," Mom said. "Quite impressive. I can see how building it must've taken a lot of work."

"Yes," I agreed. "So that's the sort of stuff we've been up to. You don't need to worry. If I actually thought Waylon was going to trap a bobcat, I would've said something, and Dad too."

Mom laughed. "I almost wish I could've seen how things played out with that skunk."

I shook my head and laughed along with her.

"You know, your father and Uncle Rusty spent countless hours exploring those woods when they were kids. Your escapades have brought back good memories for him."

I nodded.

"I suppose that's why I'm going to let this continue, but no more sneaking out. As your mother, I want to know where you're going, when you're going, and who you're with. And I want to know when you get home. That's never going to change, so you might as well get used to it."

"Okay," I agreed.

"And I know your father stressed to come to us if you ever need help with anything. Anything at all. And I want to make sure you know that's still the case."

"Yes," I said.

"Good." She hugged me then. "You can get your brother and go. And please, be safe."

"Promise," I said.

In hindsight, I'm not sure I would've said that if I'd known what Waylon had in mind for my rite of passage. Because like I said, there was no way I could back out. No. Matter. What.

44

LORETTA

My Challenge, Revealed

We were late getting to Louie's, but that didn't matter. He was ready and waiting. He slipped out a first-floor window and met us in the underbrush behind his house after spotting our headlamps. No ladder and no trickery this time.

"Let's go," he urged, keeping his voice low.

There was so much to say, but we saved talking until we reached the fortress and settled around the Circle of Stones. Waylon got right to work building our fire, the stench of skunk still lingering in the air.

"We didn't know if you'd be able to make it," I said to Louie, breaking the ice.

"I was hoping you'd come tonight. I pleaded with the Forest Spirits to send you."

Waylon smiled at the mention of the Forest Spirits.

"It's been hard staying away," I said, casting my brother a sideways glare, "after what happened last time."

Louie nodded. "My mom's been on high alert since she caught you, constantly scanning the yard, refusing to sleep. I begged the spirits to keep you away until it was safe. Thankfully, with the help of her pills, she finally crashed a few hours ago."

"Why does your mom need the pills?" Waylon asked, unable to keep that question in any longer.

"To keep the nightmares away," Louie replied.

"Nightmares? Of what?"

"I don't know. Just nightmares. There's no time for this. We must proceed, and our first order of business is honoring Trapper Waylon." Louie rose to his feet, taking us by surprise. He had plans.

"Many champions and great warriors have said that while the result matters, it's the journey one takes in trying to get there that is truly important," he began. "It is for that very reason we celebrate Trapper Waylon. For even though you did not catch the elusive bobcat, that was not because of lack of will or effort. If anything, your relentless pursuit is seen as inspiring. The Forest Spirits are not frowning; they are looking upon you with admiration."

Listening to Louie talk, I began to wonder, *How did we even get here?* (That was something I'd ponder more before we got done this summer.) I wished there was a camera crew with us, because we would've made one good movie.

Waylon stood, his face highlighted by the glow from the flames. "I appreciate your remarks," he said. "Thank you. But I can only move on after fully conquering the challenge presented to me, and I did not do that. The Forest Spirits will offer me another opportunity when the time is right, and when they do, I'll be ready."

"Another opportunity to trap the bobcat?" Louie asked, his voice cracking a bit.

"No," Waylon replied. "A wildlife animal patrol group was able to capture and relocate the bobcat. It'll need to be a new challenge."

"You mean the bobcat is no longer in our area?" Louie asked.

"That's right," Waylon confirmed.

"Phew," Louie replied, not even trying to hide his relief.

It didn't matter how mad Waylon and I were, Louie's reaction made both of us crack a smile because Captain Camo was the one who was trying to be all serious and strong. It took him a second, but after learning the bobcat was out of the picture, Louie was able to regain his composure.

"We accept your position and await your next challenge," Captain Camo said to my brother. "In the meantime, we present you with a small gift."

A gift? Really? These two never ran out of ideas.

Louie went to his pack and pulled out the surprise. When he turned back around, he held a coonskin hat in his hands. *Where did he get that thing?!* I wondered.

"Heroic explorers sometimes wore these," Louie said. "It's time you have your own. You've earned it."

Waylon was all smiles. He took the hat and slipped

in on. It was a tad big for his head and looked goofy, but it was perfect. Waylon's chest swelled. I'd hoped Louie's thoughtfulness would soften my brother up so he'd go easy on me with the rite of passage—but so much for wishful thinking.

"I'm honored," Waylon said. "Thank you."

Louie wasn't quite done. He pulled a new harmonica—new, meaning one we hadn't seen before—from his pocket and began to play. He chose a lively tune for this occasion. In response, Waylon danced around the fire, keeping one hand on his head to stop the coonskin hat from falling into his eyes. The celebration didn't last long, but it counted.

When Louie's playing came to an end, so did the dancing. Waylon took over at that point.

"The Forest Spirits have brought us together under this majestic night for another reason," he announced. "Loretta, it's time for your rite of passage."

Louie gasped. "But I thought we got to make up our own!" he cried.

"The Forest Spirits chose to reveal Loretta's to me," Waylon explained. "Call it the twin connection. It cannot be ignored."

"Relax, Louie," I said. "This challenge is for me, not you."

With all the confident pretending I was doing, I could've won an Academy Award, but what choice did I have? As the fearless leader, as the wolf, and especially because of our fight, I needed to be brave and accept whatever challenge my brother had for me. No matter what.

Waylon took a deep breath. "Loretta, you must count coup for your rite of passage."

"What?" Louie didn't understand.

Neither did I.

"To count coup was the greatest achievement for the Plains Indians," Waylon continued. "This was accomplished by performing incredible acts of bravery in the face of the enemy, with the highest honor going to those that touched the enemy warrior and then escaped unharmed."

My breathing had quickened along with my heart rate, but I remained still and stone-faced.

"Your rite of passage is to count coup," Waylon repeated.

"Wait, I'm confused," Louie interrupted. "I don't get it. Who's the enemy she has to touch?"

Waylon didn't respond. He didn't need to. P.E. Bubba and Leon Hurd were formidable adversaries, but they weren't nearby, and they weren't the scariest. That left only one option.

"Who's the enemy?" Louie asked again.

"Your mother," I whispered.

Louie gasped.

"She's not really an enemy," Waylon was quick to clarify. "Don't take it the wrong way. But she does present a certain risk."

"A certain risk? You're crazy!" Louie cried. "You saw her. If my mother catches Loretta, she'll—"

"Exactly," Waylon said. "It has to be dangerous in order for it to qualify as counting coup and for it to be considered as Loretta's rite of passage."

"No, it's—" Louie tried protesting again.

"I'll do it," I said, silencing them.

45

WAYLON

What Have I Done?

This counting-coup idea had come to me when I was at my maddest, after Loretta had said those things about Penelope and about me not really being Louie's friend. I was so angry I never stopped to consider the danger involved. I told myself I didn't care because I thought I hated my sister. But this was real. There was definitely danger. Except I couldn't call it off. Not now. No matter what.

I extinguished the fire, and then the three of us gathered our things and set out for Louie's house. I led the way, not slowing until we reached the edge of the woods. At its scariest, the nighttime forest was still nothing compared to what my sister was about to try. We stopped and crouched in the underbrush, scoping out the scene. Louie puffed his inhaler.

"It looks clear," I said.

Loretta nodded.

"Remember, the spirits are with you," I reminded her.

She inched forward, preparing to leave, but Louie grabbed her arm. "Enter through that window," he said, pointing, suddenly finding his voice. "It's the one I came out, so it'll be unlocked. My mother has night-lights throughout the house, so don't bother with your head-lamp."

Loretta was itching to go, but Louie's instructions were important.

"You'll need to cross through a few rooms and go up the stairs. My mom's bedroom is at the end of the hall-way."

"Okay. Got it," she replied. Again, she turned to leave, but Louie still had her arm.

"Loretta, this isn't a joke," he warned. "If my mother catches you . . . I don't know what'll happen. Please be careful."

If she wasn't scared before, there was a good chance she was now. I was—so much so that I licked my lips and was about to call the whole thing off.

"I'll be right back. Don't worry," she said.

I didn't know if she truly believed that or not, but she was gone, racing toward the window Louie had indicated. I watched as my sister disappeared into the enemy's lair— and I was more scared then than I'd ever been. *What have I done?* I worried.

"I should've told her not to touch anything. My mother will notice if anything is out of place," Louie moaned.

"She won't make that mistake," I assured him. "Trust me. Loretta has seen enough movies to know better." And that was the truth.

My reassurance seemed to do the trick because Louie didn't say anything more. Either that, or he was too nervous to speak. So that was it. We stayed hunkered down in the cover of the underbrush, not talking, just waiting— and rooting for Loretta. Hoping she made it out alive.

46

LORETTA

Counting Coup

I slid the window up and stepped through the opening, my hands gently holding the blinds to keep them from rattling and banging against the frame. Once inside, I took in my surroundings. There was a small table and chairs set in the middle of the room and a tall hutch against one wall, nothing too exciting or out of the ordinary—except for the exact placement of the chairs and the meticulous arrangement of the china behind the glass doors of the hutch. Every piece was in order and lined up just so, as were the picture frames sitting on the surface beneath the doors. The display was perfect.

I took a breath and made my first step. Then my second. I continued moving, maintaining laser focus on the doorway leading into the next room. I didn't make it far before my mistake caught up to me. I'd thought leaving the window open was a good idea because it would make for a quicker escape, should I need it. However, what I failed to realize was that it also meant a breeze could blow through the house—and that's exactly what happened, except this breeze was more of a gust, and it knocked over one of the pictures.

The sudden noise scared me so bad that I almost died on the spot. I practically jumped out of my skin. Luckily, I also covered my mouth and managed to trap my horror-movie scream before it escaped. My body buzzed with whatever chemicals rush around inside you after you get scared to death. I stood there, shaking, heart hammering, listening for any indication that Louie's mother was now awake. I didn't move an inch, terrified that I might not be alone anymore.

After a few minutes of continued silence, my heart slowed. I thanked my lucky stars and the Forest Spirits too, and then I pulled myself together and kept going. I had to. I didn't have time to waste. The longer I took, the riskier this got.

I walked around the table to the hutch, intending to lay the rest of the pictures flat before any others accidentally fell. I'd fix them before leaving—if all went well. If it didn't, fixing the pictures would be the least of my worries.

I grasped the first frame but stopped short before setting it down. It was a shot of Louie's parents cuddling on a beach at sunset, arms wrapped around each other. Next to that one was a picture of Louie's dad pushing him on a Big Wheel when he was a little boy. I picked up the frame that had fallen. It was a photo of Louie's father playing the harmonica. I looked from one image to the next and back again. My mind raced with possibilities, but I would need to ponder them later. I had to keep going.

I laid the pictures flat and made my way into the kitchen. Again, nothing out of the ordinary—except for the single place setting at the table, perfectly arranged with every utensil in order and cloth napkin delicately folded.

From there, I peeked around the corner into the living room. It appeared to be empty, but I could only see the back of the couch. I'd seen too many scary movies to make that costly mistake. I got down on my belly and army crawled across the floor. Louie would've appreciated my effort. Slowly, I rose to my knees and peered over the top of the couch. I sighed with relief when I found nothing more than pillows. Then I caught sight of the adjacent end table and picture standing on it—this one of the young couple dancing at their wedding.

So many questions. *Keep going,* I told myself.

I got to my feet and tiptoed to the stairs. It was time to find her bedroom, where I hoped with all hope, she was still fast asleep. If not . . . I didn't even want to think about that.

As silent as a hunter moving through the forest—my brother, who was angry with me, would've been proud—I crept up the steps and down the hall. Thankfully, the door at the end wasn't latched. Gently, I eased it open but only to the point where I could slide my body through the gap. I didn't want to nudge it any farther than needed in case it creaked. If you've seen as many movies as I have, then you know doors do that.

Here goes nothing, I thought. *Time to play Mission: Impossible.*

I slipped through the opening and stepped inside my enemy's quarters. The first thing I noticed were the piles of wadded tissues strewn about the bed and littering the floor. Perched atop the nightstand were an empty wine bottle and glass. And next to that, yet another photo, this one of Louie's father dressed in army gear—waving goodbye. I grimaced and looked back at the woman passed out under a blanket in the middle of it all. I stared at her.

Touch the enemy and get out, I told myself. *Count coup.*

I knelt and crawled across the floor. I reached her bedside and inched my way closer to the sleeping woman. All I had to do was touch her and retreat. That was it. Count coup and run—but I couldn't.

I was stopped by the letter that she'd fallen asleep holding in her hand. I couldn't read all of the words, only the last few sentences because the writing had gone onto the back of the page.

Can't wait to be home with you and Louie for Christmas. Miss you both. I love you.

It was from Louie's father. The envelope lying nearby was postmarked from more than a year ago. The story I'd been piecing together since seeing the first set of pictures downstairs had to be true. I swallowed, fighting the knot in my throat.

Looking at Louie's mother now, she wasn't the same wild and crazy woman. She wasn't scary at all. She was sad—deeply sad. The love of her life never made it home. And now she chased her sorrows away with wine and fought the nightmares with sleeping pills. I wished there was something I could do for her.

And then it happened. Waylon would say the Forest Spirits spoke to me, and maybe he's right, but whatever it was, the answer just hit me. You know that scene in the movie when the lead actress has that breakthrough moment and everything suddenly becomes clear and makes sense to her, like in Disney's *Tangled,* when Rapunzel discovers *she's* the lost princess. Or in *Dumbo* when the elephant figures out it's not the feather that makes him fly. An epiphany, that's what it's called. I had an epiphany. I suddenly understood that it wasn't my brother who needed my help any longer, but Louie's mom. She definitely wasn't the enemy. She was just a heartbroken woman.

A tingling sensation raced through my body. Goose bumps sprang up all over my skin. I needed to leave a sign—but how? And what? I glanced around the bedroom, thinking, looking for anything that might help. And then I reverted to the thing that always helps me when I need to figure something out. I thought of all the movies I'd ever watched, searching for what happens in a moment like this, and the answer came to me.

I crept into the adjoining bathroom. As I'd hoped, I found a tube of lipstick in one of the vanity drawers. In dark red letters, I wrote CALL FOR HELP—AND A JOB! across the mirror. Below that, I added Dad's name and phone number. *Nothing like killing two birds with one stone,* I thought, and smiled. My father needed an assistant and Louie's mother needed my father's help.

I stepped back and looked at the glass. There was no way she could miss it. Louie's mother just needed to call, which I knew was much easier said than done. That was why making it happen was going to be up to someone else.

My work here was done. There was only one thing left to do. I crawled back to her bedside and gently touched her forearm, officially counting coup. She didn't move. Don't ask me why, but then I did something truly risky—and maybe even dumb. I took things one step further and leaned down and whispered into her ear, "Make the call," hoping she might remember hearing those words in her sleep and believe it was a voice from somewhere else—or someone else.

Louie's mother never moved, but I did. Like a Jedi Knight, I slipped out of the bedroom and back down the stairs. I fixed the pictures on the hutch and snuck out the same window that I'd come in, remembering to close it behind me.

Then I turned and ran. It was time to tell Louie that his rite of passage awaited him.

47

LORETTA

The Truth About Louie's Father

I ducked behind cover and bent over huffing and puffing from my sprint across the yard.

"You made it," Waylon said, and sighed.

He sounded relieved. I knew I was.

"Did you do it?" he asked tentatively. "Did you count coup?"

I nodded.

"You did? You really did it!" Now he sounded a mix of amazed and excited.

"Yes," I said, "and I brought this to prove it." I straightened and showed them the tube of lipstick I held in my hand.

"Whoa," Waylon murmured, clearly impressed.

Louie looked stricken with fear. "You didn't take anything else, or move or touch anything else, did you?"

"No," I replied. "Don't worry, I noticed how perfect and precise your mom keeps everything—like that place setting on the kitchen table."

His gaze fell to the ground.

"You know what else I noticed? There are a lot of pictures in your house. Pictures of you and your mother—and your father." I paused. Waylon glanced back and forth between Louie and me, trying to make sense of what he was hearing, but Louie didn't budge. "I needed something that I could write with," I continued, "and I found this lipstick in your mom's bathroom. I used it to leave a message on her mirror."

Waylon's reaction was one of pure alarm. "You what?!" he exclaimed.

Louie looked up at me then. "You left her a message?" he croaked. "What did it say?"

I answered his question with *the* question. "Louie, what happened to your father?"

His eyes grew wet almost instantly. He blinked several times and swallowed, then went back to staring at the ground. He scuffed his foot across the dirt. Waylon and I waited. There was more mindless scuffing, but eventually, Louie started talking.

"My father was a combat medic," he began. "He was the guy who went into battle with the troops so he could help all the fallen soldiers. He always said it was an honor to be there for the men and women who put their lives on the line to protect the freedoms most of us take for granted."

Waylon glanced at me, beginning to understand.

"He went on a lot of deployments over the years," Louie continued, "but he didn't make it back home from the last one. The jeep he was riding in on his way to the hospital hit a land mine. They say he didn't suffer. Everyone died on impact."

"I'm sorry," I whispered.

"I know," he rasped.

"The harmonica was from your dad, wasn't it?" Waylon said. "And the camouflage and your medical kit too. And you learned your skills from him?"

"Yeah," he replied, scuffing at the dirt again.

"Louie, I found something else in your house," I said.

His foot stopped. He looked up at me, confused.

"Your rite of passage," I explained.

He glanced at Waylon, but the only thing my brother could offer were raised eyebrows and a shrug. Waylon had no idea what I was talking about.

"Louie, your mother needs help," I continued. "She's depressed, and she's not getting any better."

"She's grieving, that's all. She just needs more time."

He could go on trying to convince himself of that lie, but it wasn't working on me.

"No," I said, firmer than I meant, but I knew I was right. "She might still be grieving, but she's also depressed, and she won't get better unless she gets help. You can't do this on your own. And you shouldn't have to."

Louie's gaze fell to the ground again. He wasn't going to argue because he knew the truth.

"Getting your mother to admit she needs help, and convincing her to seek it, is your rite of passage," I said. "You have to do it."

He sniffled and wiped his nose, then lifted his chin and looked at me through wet eyes, shaking his head and shrugging. "What if I can't?"

"You can," I reassured him.

"But how?"

"The answer is in the message I left on her mirror," I said, and began explaining. "Your mother's going to see a name and phone number—my father's. He's a psychologist. His job is counseling people—and he's in desperate need of an assistant. Somebody who can help him organize his office, and from what I saw inside your house, your mom is amazing at keeping things neat. You need to make sure she calls him."

"She wasn't always like this," Louie said, and sniffled again. "After Dad, she became superstitious, but now she's anxious about everything. I have to sneak out if I want to leave the house, and I have to do homeschooling because she's afraid to let me out of her sight. She's terrified of losing me too. She's told me so."

The more Louie revealed, the sadder I felt for him and his mom—and the more I knew I was right. "You need her to make the call," I stressed.

"We bought this old house because Mom heard the rumors about it being haunted and all," Louie continued. "She hoped this place would help her connect with Dad's spirit in the afterlife. That he might be able to cross over and visit us. My father had traveled through this area once long ago and liked it. He'd told my mom he wanted to move here one day. So . . ."

"Louie . . . you need her to make the call," I stressed

once more. "It's your rite of passage, but it's more than that. Your mother needs help. And so do you. You've got to stand up to her and make her see that."

He wiped his face.

"We'll make sure our father is ready," I promised.

Louie looked at Waylon and me with pain and sorrow behind his red eyes and weak smile. He nodded, then stepped out of the forest and walked to his house. He never glanced back. He had to go alone. That was the way it had to be with a rite of passage.

"May the force be with you," I whispered.

"And the Forest Spirits too," Waylon added.

There was no fire ceremony or special tattoos. Everything up to this point had had some element of fun—but not anymore. There was nothing fun about Louie's quest. This was much bigger now.

48

LORETTA

The Phone Call

I tiptoed into my parents' bedroom and tapped Mom on the shoulder. "We're back," I whispered, letting her know we were home as I'd promised.

She touched my hand. "Thank you, sweetie."

She turned over, and I went and found my bed after that, hoping for sleep, but there was too much racing through my mind. Was Waylon in the same boat? Was he still mad at me? Our fight seemed so long ago now—and suddenly, not so important.

I lay staring at the ceiling, hugging my pillow and worrying about Louie. At some point, my eyes finally closed.

Here was the good news. Ever since Dad had become aware of our overnight missions, he began letting Waylon and me sleep in later, agreeing to turn breakfast into brunch, because even if we were starting our days later than normal, we still had to start with a strong meal. It was only on our camp days when this wasn't possible. We still had to drag ourselves out of bed nice and early on those mornings—but a few sleep-late days were better than none, so I wasn't complaining. I saw no downside to our new arrangement until the morning after counting coup.

I woke with a start, jarred by squealing laughter—which was annoying! That was quickly followed by my father's boisterous laughter—which was concerning. Very!

I flung my covers off and ran downstairs. The kitchen was empty, except for the note left sitting on the table.

You're on your own this morning. Cereal in cabinet and muffins on the counter. I have an interview.

Love,
Dad

On cue, there was the laughter again. It was coming from Dad's office. I hurried to that end of the house and found his door ajar. I peeked through the crack. Sure enough, he was in the midst of his interview—and based on his smiles and her annoying laughter, it appeared to be going well.

No! This can't be happening! I screamed inside my head.

This was really messing with my plans. It was not good. Not good at all. If Dad hired the woman on the other side of this door, then it would be too late for Louie's mother.

I couldn't stand by and allow that to happen. I had to do something. But what?

By now you should be able to guess how I figured that out. Don't ever let your parents tell you watching TV is bad again. The answer was in a favorite movie of mine— *The Parent Trap*. Ever see it? You need to. It's great. In that movie, twin sisters team up and perform some serious sabotage to prevent their father from marrying the wrong woman. There's more that needs explaining, but what's important here is the word "sabotage." And also "twin," because I had one of those too—if he didn't still hate me.

I turned and ran. Time was short. I burst into my brother's room.

"Waylon, get up!" I urged.

He sat bolt upright like a rocket. "Huh? What? What's wrong?"

"We have an emergency. Get up and get dressed."

He stumbled out of bed, still half-asleep, and began rummaging through the clothes that littered his floor. He kicked his dirty socks and underwear out of the way— gross! How did I know they were dirty? Double gross! But then an idea came to me.

I grabbed his laundry basket and filled it with every piece of clothing strewn about, and then I topped it off with Waylon's best tire-track underwear. Don't worry, I gloved my hand in one of his shirts before touching those things.

"Hey, I've been looking for this," Waylon exclaimed after discovering the hand buzzer previously buried. I'd given it to him for Christmas a few years back, after he'd read Harry Potter and wanted us to open a joke shop like Fred and George Weasley—also twins.

"See what happens when you clean your room," I said.

He stuck his tongue out at me.

"Bring the buzzer," I said. "It'll be a nice additional touch."

"Why? What're we doing?" he asked, fully awake now.

I quickly filled him in, and then he grabbed his favorite joke item. I was nervous, but Waylon was excited to do damage. Together, we hurried back downstairs to Dad's office. I heard that squealing laugh again before we even got there—which should've been reason enough not to hire this lady. It was time for sabotage!

I barged in, throwing Dad's door wide open. Let me remind you of his one cardinal rule: Unless there's a fire or someone is dying, NEVER interrupt him when he's with someone in his office.

But this someone wasn't a patient; she was simply the wrong person for the job. And I had to make sure *she* knew that.

"Ohh!" the startled woman cried. "You have children!"

"Yes, I do," Dad replied, his jaw clenching. "And I have no clue why they're here."

"There's two of us. Double trouble," I responded with a wink.

"We're twins," Waylon said, offering the woman his hand for a shake. "I'm Waylon."

She placed her hand in his, and he grabbed on with a firm grip. Boy, did she get zapped good!

"Ohh!" she cried.

"Gotcha," Waylon said, and laughed.

"Waylon! Loretta!" Dad scolded. "What do you think you're doing? You know not to interrupt me when I'm in a meeting."

"So here's our laundry," I said to the woman, slapping the basket on her lap, my brother's skiddsters just under her nose. "I'm sure my dad has already covered this part of the job."

"No, I'm afraid he hasn't," she replied, recoiling from Waylon's trophy.

"Loretta!" Dad thundered again. "You're out of line."

The woman in the chair glanced from me to Dad. She was at a loss.

"When you're done with that, can you make me some chicken noodle soup? I'm not feeling well," Waylon said to her next.

She didn't know how to respond.

"Taking care of us is the most important part of the job," I told her.

Waylon began rubbing his belly, and then he unloaded, throwing fake vomit all over the basket and her lap.

"Ohh!" she screamed in horror. The woman sprang from her chair, dumping the basket and brushing off her lap. "Dr. Neal, thank you for your time, but I'm no longer interested in this position."

And just like that, she was gone. Dad didn't even respond. There was nothing for him to say. He watched his interviewee run away, and then he turned on us. "You need to leave," he growled. "I'm much too angry to discuss what just happened with you now."

"Dad, I'm sorry, but—" I started, trying to explain.

"Leave," he said, unwilling to listen.

"Dad."

"Now!" he exploded.

Waylon and I gathered up the laundry basket and vomit. Explaining anything to our father would need to wait until later. We kept our mouths shut and left without another word—almost. We were only a few steps from the doorway when his phone rang, stopping us dead in our tracks.

"Louie," I whispered.

"You think so?" Waylon replied.

I dropped the basket and hurried back across the room.

"I said leave," Dad warned.

When his phone rang the second time, I saw the name listed on caller ID. "Dad, you have to answer it. That woman wasn't the one for the job, but the person calling right now is. She's superb at organization, has experience as an administrative assistant (I didn't know if that was true, but it sounded good), and she needs *your* help."

A third ring. He looked at me, his hard glare melting away and turning into confusion.

"I'm coming to you now like you asked—because I can't do this without you. Please."

A fourth ring. There was so much to explain, but no time.

"Trust the Forest Spirits," Waylon said, arriving by my side.

"Please," I said softly.

A fifth ring—Dad reached over and picked up. "Hello . . . This is he. . . . Yes, I am. . . . Yes . . . That is also true. . . . I see. Well, can you come by this afternoon? . . . That'll work. I look forward to seeing you then."

He hung up and looked at us. "You two better sit down. You have some explaining to do."

49

LORETTA

Explaining

Our explaining started with us befriending Louie after meeting him unexpectedly.

"You'd love him, Dad. He's big. Real big. And real nice. And he always wears camouflage," Waylon said, rattling off information about our best friend.

"We'll get to the camouflage," I said, trying to slow my brother down.

"He prefers jazz," Waylon added. "His father named him after Louis Armstrong. But your country might work if it's got a harmonica in it. You should hear Louie play the harmonica."

"I don't understand," Dad said. "If this boy is your friend, why were you sneaking into his house?"

I put my hands up. "We'll get there," I promised. "All of this is important."

"Does this have anything to do with your adventure game?"

"Patience," I said.

Finally, after getting him and Waylon to take a breath, I took the lead and began explaining about our mission to the Millennium Falcon and discovering a mysterious cigar box wrapped in cloth and bound shut.

"You told me about finding game directions, not a cigar box," Dad interrupted.

"There was a note in the box," I said, "along with some other stuff."

"What other stuff?" he asked, growing agitated.

"Just stuff." I was trying to avoid the dirty-magazine detail.

"I want to see it."

"It's not important."

"I want to see it!" he demanded, his voice rising.

I turned to my brother. "It's at the fortress," Waylon said. "I can run and get it."

"Yes," Dad insisted. "Go."

Waylon didn't hesitate. He sprang from his seat and was gone in a flash.

I wondered why Dad was so interested in the cigar box but not enough to stop and ask. I was too focused on telling him our story so he was ready for Louie's mother, Ms. Foster. I pressed ahead and continued bringing him up to speed, recapping our sacrifices and Waylon's rite of passage.

"Yes, I know about all of that," Dad said, sounding irritated, "but that still doesn't tell me why you're suddenly breaking and entering into houses."

"I was sneaking in, not breaking and entering," I corrected him. "And you may think you know about all of that, but you don't know everything."

He scowled. "What does that mean?"

This was where I began telling him about Louie's mom, starting with the night she caught us holding the ladder as Louie climbed back into his bedroom. I told him about all the things Louie had said about his mother leading up to that moment.

"And you thought sneaking into her house would be a good idea?" Dad asked. "Based on what you've just told me, I'd say that was a reckless and extremely dangerous decision."

"My frontal lobe isn't fully developed yet," I replied, which actually made him smirk for just a second.

"That doesn't excuse what you did," he countered.

"It was my rite of passage. I was counting coup."

Dad sat back. "So this was your brother's idea?"

I shrugged.

"And what made him think of it?"

I shrugged again. "I don't know. He came home from camp with the idea." That wasn't the whole truth, but I didn't feel like telling him about the fight we'd had.

Dad shook his head and let out a heavy breath. Was he disappointed? "Loretta, we're not done talking about this, not by a long shot, but I still don't understand why Louie's mother called me this morning and why you're convinced she's the person I need to hire?"

I filled him in on everything I'd seen inside her house, detailing the pictures, the wine, and the letter she held in her hand. I also took time to tell him how immaculate she kept the place. And then I described the message I'd left for her on the bathroom mirror and, lastly, the history Louie shared with us after I'd returned from counting coup—about the house and spirits and his mother.

Dad sighed. His expression softened. "Your mother told me about your secret plan concerning your brother."

"I knew she would. You two aren't good at keeping secrets from each other. And you proved that wasn't a good idea."

Dad chuckled. "Yeah, I guess I did. But that's not what's important here. Loretta, you've proven that your heart is bigger than your fists. You've always been protective of your brother, but what you've done for Louie and his mom is all heart."

"You told me not to do anything you wouldn't do."

He smiled.

It's possible I would've told Dad about my fight with Waylon and why I was feeling so uneasy, but my brother returned before any of that happened. He walked in carrying the cigar box, and there's really no other way to describe it—my father looked like he'd just seen a ghost.

50

LORETTA

More Explaining

Waylon handed the box to Dad and sat next to me. We watched in silence as our father flipped the latch on the front and lifted the top. "Oh my God."

You've heard enough at this point to know my father was more of the sensitive type than a fighter, but I'd still never seen him cry—not until that moment. His eyes welled up as he touched the rabbit's foot. He smiled through the tears when he came to Buzz Lightyear. I panicked when I recalled the dirty magazine, expecting him to pull that out of the box next, but then I remembered I'd confiscated it and I relaxed.

"Do you have the note?" Dad rasped, wiping his face.

Waylon passed the paper to him. My brother and I still hadn't said a word. We braced ourselves for what might happen after Dad read the letter. What happened was not anything I was expecting.

My father lost control and began all-the-way crying. I'm talking sobs and body-shaking stuff. I can tell you this, when you witness something like that, your mind races, searching for answers. The explanation came to me all at once in what could only be described as my second Rapunzel epiphany.

"Dad, what was Uncle Rusty's middle name?" I asked.

"Owen," he croaked.

Waylon's mouth fell open. My brother understood now too. RON wasn't anyone's name. Those letters were my uncle Rusty's initials, Rusty Owen Neal.

"That note was meant for you, wasn't it?" I said.

Dad nodded and sniffled. "Yes . . . but it was my children, my own daredevils, who found it. Talk about Forest Spirits."

Daredevils, I thought. That was the perfect name for our club.

Waylon beamed.

"Your uncle and I smoked cigars from this very box on his last night before he left for boot camp," Dad said after wiping his face again.

"You smoked a cigar?" Waylon exclaimed, sounding both incredulous and impressed.

"Only time," Dad made clear. "It was awful, so don't try it, but Rusty wanted me to join him. . . . Maybe he knew . . . ," Dad mused, his voice trailing off.

"Tell us about the things Uncle Rusty put in the box," Waylon said, eager to hear the stories behind our uncle's sentimental artifacts.

So Dad began—and Waylon and I were captivated. We heard more about Uncle Rusty than we ever knew. It was Dad who gave his brother the rabbit's foot for good luck before Uncle Rusty went off to the army, but it seemed now that Uncle Rusty wanted to leave that luck with Dad—and Waylon and me. The cassette tape was one Uncle Rusty made of Johnny Cash and that he played over and over when they were young. That tape was what got Dad hooked on country. (I found out later that Johnny Cash's older brother died when he was a boy, and that connection was something Dad felt with the Man in Black.)

The Buzz Lightyear piece was my favorite story and had my eyes wet by the end. Dad and Uncle Rusty were at the lake one summer day when a little girl started calling for help. She'd gone out too far on her raft and couldn't make it back when the raft went flat. Uncle Rusty was only sixteen years old, but he heard her cries and swam out and rescued her. Dad said the girl was terrified and left marks all over Uncle Rusty from where her nails had dug into his skin. When they reached the beach, that little girl's brother gave Uncle Rusty his Buzz Lightyear for being a real superhero. Uncle Rusty took the toy but never made a big deal out of what he'd done. In fact, he never told anyone.

It's hard to sum up everything I felt and learned sitting with Waylon and my dad that morning. There was an element of Cinderella in our story. The way she'd snuck to the ball and the way Waylon and I had been sneaking out, the magic of the fairy godmother and the mystery of the Forest Spirits, and how a simple glass slipper or an old wooden cigar box could bring all the pieces together in the end. Okay, maybe not. What can I say? It was probably *The Goonies* that captured us best again—because of the way family is celebrated.

So much had just happened for my father. Thanks to a cigar box and note, and his children, he'd reconnected with Uncle Rusty. And there was so much yet to come for Louie and his mother. Like I said, family.

But first things first. Turns out the Forest Spirits had more in store for the Daredevils. Mom came home for lunch, surprising us, and surprising us even more when she asked Waylon and me if we knew anything about the email all the parents of campers had received, something about a garbage-can fiasco that had damaged P.E. Bubba's car.

"You mean the car catcher?" Waylon corrected her, which wasn't a great first move.

CLOSING
SCENES

CHAPTER 51

LORETTA

The Great Horned Owl's Chicken Dance

Waylon, Louie, and I sat around the Circle of Stones. It was our first midnight meeting since everything went down. There was no sneaking out required this time.

Ms. Foster, who was okay with us calling her Ella, was officially Dad's assistant and things were already improving—most notably, Dad's office. Ella had his space organized and under control in a matter of days. But more important, with Dad's help, Ms. Foster was on the road to getting better. It would be a long road, Dad had reminded us, but she was on her way.

Aiding in Ms. Foster's trip to getting better was the fact that she and Mom had become good friends. The two of them struck it off from the start, sorta like Louie and Waylon and me. Mom was happy to spend time with Louie's mother outside of work so that Ms. Foster wasn't always alone. She said Ella's jazz music was a nice break from Dad's country.

What about Louie? His mom was still terrified of

losing him like she had her husband, but Ms. Foster was trying hard to let go. To let Louie live. By that, I mean she was allowing him to spend time with Waylon and me. And the real big news, Louie would be attending school with us in the fall!

Needless to say, Louie and I had succeeded in our rites of passage, which explains why we found ourselves gathered around the Circle of Stones again. My brother was adamant our victories called for a fire ceremony or we risked upsetting the Forest Spirits. We had reason to celebrate.

Waylon used Uncle Rusty's lighter and brought our fire to life. As the flames grew, I began wondering what my brother would propose for a final round of tattoos, but before we got to that point, something truly unexpected took us by surprise. We had a visitor.

"Dad?" Waylon said. "What're you doing here?"

"The Forest Spirits have spoken to me. I need to join your fire ceremony this evening."

The three of us glanced at each other and shrugged.

"Okay," Waylon said, smirking. "Our fire ceremonies always begin with tattoos." He lifted his pant leg to reveal his rabbit and then showed off the eagle on his shoulder as examples. "You must step over here to receive yours."

Dad played along. He stood where Waylon indicated and rolled up his sleeve. Waylon prepped the area and then uncapped his marker and began drawing. It wasn't his best work because he didn't have anything to trace from paper. We didn't know Dad would be coming so

Waylon had to improvise, but he did a good job. I could tell what it was that he'd drawn—and it was perfect.

When he finished, Waylon capped the marker and made his announcement. "You've been given the great horned owl to represent your advanced age. May the Forest Spirits continue to pass along wisdom as you grow even older and grayer."

Louie and I laughed.

Dad sneered but didn't object.

"We're not quite finished," Waylon said. "Since you come with a message from the Forest Spirits, we must give you stripes." He took the marker and added two swipes under Dad's left eye, and then two under his right. "Now you're ready. Dance."

Dad's face scrunched.

"Around the fire," Waylon emphasized. "Dance."

Dad started, and I burst into laughter. Our fire ceremony had just turned into comedy hour. Dad's movements resembled a chicken dance, not any owl. After poking fun, we joined to help him out, Waylon first, and then Louie and me. It was an energetic dance, made even better when Waylon got near Louie and me and let us in on his secret.

"I used my permanent markers," he whispered.

Oh. My. God. That was all I needed to hear, and I was cracking up again. Dad was going to spend the next month looking like a raccoon!

We continued dancing and laughing our way around the circle before finally coming to a stop. Dad laughed with us. He was a good sport. He was also clueless because he wouldn't be laughing come morning when he couldn't get those stripes off.

"Daredevils, I've joined you tonight for a very special reason," Dad said, turning serious. "I come with a gift."

We took seats and quieted, curious to see what he'd brought. But before the gift, Dad first shared a story with us.

"Many years ago, my brother died while in the service," he began. "When his body came home, he was accompanied by a few friends. They spoke about Rusty, but I was too pained to listen to everything they said—my hero was gone. I may not remember the words they shared, but I will forever remember the song that was played on this harmonica."

Dad pulled the small instrument from his pocket and held it out. He continued.

"The harmonica-playing medic filled the air with a song that he said was Rusty's favorite. He intended to have Rusty buried with the harmonica, but I asked him if I could have it. I don't know why, but I did. I think maybe because music was something Rusty and I loved together."

Dad paused and swallowed, then looked at Louie. "Your mother mentioned your father's name in one of our sessions. Johnathan Lee Foster, is that right?"

Louie nodded.

Dad handed him the harmonica, the initials JLF scratched on the side.

"Louie, that medic was your father. I met him all those years ago. He was a great friend of my brother's."

Louie ran his finger over the side of the harmonica. He squeezed the piece of metal in his hands as his eyes filled with tears. "Thank you, Mr. Neal," he croaked.

"The Forest Spirits have wound their magic all around and in between you daredevils. The three of you were meant to find each other," Dad said.

Louie lifted his father's harmonica to his lips and began playing. I will never again doubt the power of what you can't see or explain—because it is real. I felt it.

52

LORETTA

Finding My Way

Leaving the forest that night I wondered if witnessing all that had happened for Louie and my father was my gift for a successful rite of passage. That was all I needed, and I mean that. Sure, I would've taken more screen time, but I wasn't some ungrateful brat.

It's just . . . well, I wondered. Louie had presented Waylon with a coonskin hat and my brother hadn't even succeeded in his rite of passage—according to himself. And the harmonica was an incredible gift for Louie. So a tiny piece of me wondered, *What about me?*

Go ahead and say what you want, but my wondering made me consider that maybe I wasn't done yet. That maybe there was something more I needed to do. And I knew just what that was. Finding my way started with me speaking the truth.

When we got back home, I followed my brother into his bedroom. "Waylon," I croaked. I waited for him to turn around and look at me. "I'm sorry I said those things about you and Penelope."

His face softened. "It's okay. I'm sorry too."

"I got jealous and that made me say those hurtful things that I didn't mean or believe."

"It's okay," he said again. "I didn't mean the things I said either. You're good at making friends when you're not worrying about me—and when you keep your temper in check."

I snorted. "I guess I'm a bit like Ms. Foster—too protective."

"You're not Ms. Foster. You're the wolf, and you'll always be my best friend."

That got to me a little bit when he said that, but before I could say anything more, my brother showed me just how much he was like our sentimental father. He came closer and pulled me into a hug. The hug surprised me, but not as much as the difference I felt in Waylon's arms. He was definitely stronger now. My Mr. Miyagi exercises had made a difference after all! Don't worry, the sentimental stuff didn't last long. He was still my same brother, and he proved that when he let go and stepped back.

"Tomorrow I'll be attempting my second rite of passage," he informed me.

"Tomorrow?" I said, caught off guard. "Tomorrow we have to do community service for the car catcher," I reminded him.

"I know—and before we're done, I'll approach our nemesis, P.E. Bubba, and propose a truce."

53

WAYLON

Community Service

Loretta filled in most of the details for Mom and Dad after the email about the car catcher came (leaving out Penelope). She told me I couldn't talk because I was still too excited about the trap and would wind up saying too much—which was probably true.

According to his email, P.E. Bubba did not know who was responsible. At least, he couldn't prove it, though he had his suspicions. He urged parents to talk to their children, and if anyone had any information about who was behind the heinous crime, to please report it. Luckily, insurance would be covering the cost of his repair job— which, truthfully, had seemed a lot worse at the time than the few minor dents and scratches it turned out to be.

Nonetheless, Mom and Dad spent time talking to us. They wanted to make sure Loretta and I understood that while the car catcher was very creative and well thought out, and something they wished they could've seen, it was a bad idea. Period. One of my best worst ideas, as

Dad put it. Somebody could've been hurt. However, my parents also couldn't deny that P.E. Bubba was a mean, petty, spiteful meathead who no doubt got what was coming to him. And they didn't even know the half of how he treated Loretta and me.

All that being said, my parents decided we didn't need to admit to anything because they just didn't see any good coming from that, which made Loretta very happy, but we also weren't off the hook. There had to be a consequence, and for something of this magnitude, Mom and Dad agreed that some form of community service seemed appropriate. So all together, we came up with the idea of holding a trash cleanup day at the youth center and throughout the neighboring community. All the bottles that were collected would be deposited and the money given to P.E. Bubba for emotional damages.

We did your standard advertising for the event, starting with an email to the families of all the campers and then a few social media posts, and I'm happy to report the result was a strong turnout. More kids showed than I was expecting. Maybe parents felt bad for P.E. or maybe they just liked the idea of having their children participate in community service, or maybe in the case of Grace and Alyssa, whom I'd never met before, they came because they liked Loretta. Whatever the reason, Loretta was relieved by the numbers because she said it made us look less guilty. I told her she could also be excited because with that many people we were actually going to make a difference and accomplish considerable cleanup—which I'm also happy to report, we did.

While the day's work was important, I was most focused on my second rite of passage. I put it into motion once the volunteers were spread out and P.E. made an appearance, which I knew he would because he'd want his money.

"P.E. Bubba, I want to apologize for the damage done to your Corvette," I said, approaching him.

"I knew it was you," he growled.

"I didn't say that," I clarified. "I simply wanted to say sorry. It's unfortunate what happened."

"Yeah, it is," he said, "and if I ever catch who was behind it, they're gonna pay."

"Oh, I was referring to the water you splashed all over me. Now, *that* was unfortunate."

He guffawed.

"I'd like to propose a truce," I said. "We can continue as enemies or bury the past and move forward in peace."

"You think I'd ever be friendly with your family? You're dumber than I thought."

"On the contrary, I'm much too smart for you, so I suggest you reconsider. Besides, I didn't say we needed to be friends, only that we agree to leave each other alone. It's an offer I encourage you to accept because I have the spirits of my uncle Rusty and medic Johnathan Lee Foster on my side."

"You're weird."

"And you're bald. Both are irrelevant. Truce," I said, holding out my hand for him to shake.

"I'm not accepting any offer of yours," he snarled.

I pulled my hand back. "That is disappointing. Since

Loretta and I are finished at the elementary school, I was truly hoping we could let bygones be bygones, but apparently not. Just so you know, I'll still be instructing my pack that you are off-limits. However, should you choose to cross any one of us, I will not be able to honor that promise. You've been warned."

"Pfft. Just so you know, one of the gym teachers at the middle school retired and I'm taking the position, so I'll be moving there with you. You've been warned."

I held his stare but didn't respond. Then I turned and walked away to rejoin my pack: Loretta, Louie, and Penelope. Louie had come with us because he was excited to meet people before school started in the fall, and Penelope refused to watch Loretta and me take the blame for something she had masterminded. No one had to force her to help.

Naturally, they each asked what my conversation with P.E. was all about. I filled them in, starting with the news that P.E. would be following us to the middle school and then making it clear our gym teacher was to be left alone. No one in the pack was allowed to break that vow unless P.E. crossed one of us first.

"Who's your pack?" Penelope asked.

Her question surprised me because in my mind that was obvious, but then I realized something. It wasn't official. "Loretta and Louie," I replied. "And you, once we hold a fire ceremony and officially welcome you to the Daredevils."

Louie smiled—and so did Loretta.

54

LORETTA

Thanks for the Cookies

Just when I thought our summer movie had played out and it was time for the credits, there was another surprise. Waylon wasn't done yet. He still had one more trick up his sleeve.

It happened a few days after our community service event. I had just finished watching *Star Wars, Episode V: The Empire Strikes Back.* Ever see it? I sure hope so. It's only the most famous surprise twist in movie history. When Darth Vader tells Luke, "I am your father." I mean, whoa! How do you top that? I didn't think it was possible, but like I said, Waylon wasn't done yet.

I closed my laptop and went to find my brother. He wasn't in his bedroom, so I walked downstairs to see if he was in the kitchen. Mom was home from work and beginning to make dinner.

"Have you seen Waylon?" I asked her.

"He just ran a plate of cookies out to the landscape boys for me. I wanted to do something nice for them because they've been doing a terrific job. I'm hoping your father gives up on his mower so we can keep using them."

Landscape boys? I thought, the word "boys" playing over in my mind. *What if?*

I ran from the kitchen and out the front door. Had my mother just fed Waylon to the lion?

My heart dropped when I saw the familiar orange T-shirt riding on the big mower. But where was his partner? Leon was nowhere to be found—and neither was my brother.

"Waylon!" I yelled, panicking.

I ran to the corner of the house and finally spotted the weed eater. It was lying on the ground, on the other side of their truck and trailer. Just the bottom part was sticking past the wheel where I could see it.

I took off, sprinting in that direction. I tore around the back of the trailer and came face to face with Leon. My fists clenched automatically.

"Where's my brother?" I growled.

"I don't know. He just dropped these off and left," Leon said, showing me the plate of cookies. "Thanks for making them."

My face scrunched. "What?"

"Waylon said you made them for me. Well, for me and my brother. Thanks."

"Uh . . . um," I stammered. I didn't know what to say. My head was spinning. At last, I settled on "You're welcome."

"You didn't need to make them to keep me quiet about P.E. Bubba," Leon said, "if that's what you were worried about. Trust me, I won't be saying anything. I can't stand that guy."

Now it was my turn to say thanks.

"My dad's friend beat him up in the high school parking lot once a long time ago," Leon went on. He grinned. "Wish I could've seen that."

I swallowed. "Yeah, me too."

"I got to see your penalty kick, though. That was pretty awesome."

Now I grinned.

"Leon!" his brother yelled from the mower. "Are you gonna flirt all day or finish with the weed eating?"

Leon's face turned red. I'm pretty sure mine did too. "I better get back to work," he said. "Thanks again for the cookies."

"Sure."

He grabbed his weed eater and started walking away.

"Hey, Leon," I called, my voice cracking.

He turned around.

"Thanks for not killing my brother when he came out here."

He laughed. "You can stop worrying about that too. No way I'm messing with him. I'm not only scared of you—I like you."

Let me tell you, those last three words shocked me more than Darth Vader's. He liked me?! What?!

Leon fired up his weed eater and got back to work, but I couldn't move. I was too stunned. I just stood there, watching him. Before disappearing around the side of our house, Leon glanced at me and smiled. I waved and smiled back, my heart still hammering away. Even after he was out of sight, my smile didn't fade.

I skipped back into the house, feeling . . . happy. Floating happy. My brother was there to greet me when I returned.

"Hurd's the man," he said, and smirked.

55

LORETTA

To Be Continued . . .

I couldn't decide if I'd done enough to get Waylon ready for middle school, but after watching him stand toe to toe with P.E. Bubba and escape unharmed, and then have the guts to face Leon Hurd, I knew I could stop worrying. It was never really about Waylon anyways. It was always about me, and getting me ready to be without my brother continually by my side.

I was ready now—thanks to the Daredevils. While I was still the wolf and would continue to look out for my pack, I knew they would have my back too.

If our saga was a Disney princess fairy tale, I might get away with saying we all lived happily ever after and let that be it, but that wasn't our style. We were more of an action-adventure movie—and we weren't done yet. Thanks to Waylon, the Daredevils had Penelope to tattoo and welcome into our club at a future fire ceremony, and though no one else knew it yet, we also had Leon Hurd to include. That was a must. He couldn't be all bad—

especially if he liked me. (Let's not forget, a little romance usually adds spice to a movie.) Besides, once Leon told me about his dad's friend, I knew it had to happen. Leon was connected with us through the work of the Forest Spirits.

This final scene was more of a beginning—because there were still plenty of adventures ahead. (More on that later.)

Acknowledgments

This story sat with me for a very long time and might never have become a book if it weren't for my incredible editor, Françoise Bui. As always, your insights and feedback were invaluable. I'm especially thankful for your stamina in dealing with my many nitpicky questions during copyediting. The Daredevils would honor you with a fire ceremony!

Thanks to Julie McLaughlin for the awesome cover. I love everything about it, but the animal shadows are my favorite!

I'm forever grateful for Beverly Horowitz and Paul Fedorko, two people who've been in my corner from the beginning. Big thanks to the entire publishing team at Random House Children's Books for the attention and care you continue to give to my work.

Huge hugs to my country music–loving family—for never changing the station and for singing along, even to the old stuff. And for offering advice and ideas to my random story questions—even when your answer is "I don't know." Love you all!